"Joyce Carol Oates manages to put us inside the mind of an outcast—a serial killer—and so to disturb us deeply. Depicting the worst in human nature, Oates embodies our saving virtues, empathy, imagination, and wonder. *Zombie* succeeds at a profound level, simultaneously horrifying the reader and demonstrating that nothing human is alien to us."

—Peter D. Kramer, author of
Listening to Prozac

"Enthralling . . . harrowing. . . . Oates scores aggressively with this novel."   —*Chicago Tribune*

"Oates's literary ride through the haunted house of the American psyche takes its scariest plunge yet. . . . horrifyingly effective."   —*Orlando Sentinel*

"A brilliant, horrific foray into a psychological hell."
—*Baltimore Sun*

JOYCE CAROL OATES is one of America's most celebrated writers, the author of 26 novels and numerous collections of stories, poetry, and plays. She won a National Book Award for *them*, and her 1990 novel *Because It Is Bitter and Because It Is My Heart* earned an NBA nomination. Her 1992 novel *Black Water* was nominated for the National Book Critics Circle Award and the Pulitzer Prize, and her 1994 novel *What I Lived For* was nominated for the PEN/Faulkner Award and the Pulitzer Prize. *Zombie* was awarded the 1995 Lilla Fisk Rand fiction prize by the *Boston Book Review*. Oates lives in Princeton, New Jersey, where she is the Roger S. Berlind Distinguished Professor in the Humanities at Princeton University.

Zombie

Joyce Carol Oates

A William Abrahams Book

PLUME

PLUME
Published by the Penguin Group
Penguin Books USA Inc., 375 Hudson Street,
New York, New York 10014, U.S.A.
Penguin Books Ltd, 27 Wrights Lane, London W8 5TZ, England
Penguin Books Australia Ltd, Ringwood, Victoria, Australia
Penguin Books Canada Ltd, 10 Alcorn Avenue,
Toronto, Ontario, Canada M4V 3B2
Penguin Books (N.Z.) Ltd, 182–190 Wairau Road, Auckland 10, New Zealand

Penguin Books Ltd, Registered Offices: Harmondsworth, Middlesex, England

Published by Plume, an imprint of Dutton Signet, a division of
Penguin Books USA Inc. Previously appeared in a Dutton edition.

First Plume Printing, September, 1996
10 9 8 7 6 5 4 3 2 1

 REGISTERED TRADEMARK—MARCA REGISTRADA

The Library of Congress has catalogued the Dutton edition as follows:
Oates, Joyce Carol
    Zombie / Joyce Carol Oates.
        p.   cm.
    "A William Abrahams Book."
    ISBN 0-525-94045-6 (hc.)
    ISBN 0-452-27500-8 (pbk.)
    PS3565.A8Z43   1995
    813'.54—dc20   95-8090
                             CIP

Printed in the United States of America
Designed by Leonard Telesca

PUBLISHER'S NOTE
This is a work of fiction. Names, characters, places, and incidents either are
the product of the author's imagination or are used fictitiously, and any
resemblance to actual persons, living or dead, events, or locales is entirely
coincidental.

Acknowledgments

Some of the material used in Chapter 13 is taken, in abbreviated form, from *Neuro-: Life on the Frontlines of Brain Surgery and Neurological Medicine* by David Noonan (Simon & Schuster, 1989), pp. 200–202.

Diagram used in Chapter 13 is taken from W. Freeman, *Proceedings of the Royal Society of Medicine,* 1949, 42 Suppl., pp. 8–12.

Sections of Part I appeared, in different form, in *The New Yorker,* October 1994.

Suspended Sentence

1

My name is Q__ P__ & I am thirty-one years old, three months.

Height five feet ten, weight one hundred forty-seven pounds.

Eyes brown, hair brown. Medium build. Light scattering of freckles on arms, back. Astigmatism in both eyes, corrective lenses required for driving.

Distinguishing features: none.

Except maybe these faint worm-shaped scars on both my knees. They say from a bicycle accident, I was a little boy then. I don't contradict but I don't remember.

I never contradict. I am in agreement with you as you utter your words of wisdom. Moving your asshole-mouth & YES SIR I am saying NO MA'AM I am saying. My shy eyes. Behind my plastic-rimmed glasses that are the color of skin seen through plastic.

Caucasian skin that is. On both sides of my family going back forever as far as I am aware.

My I.Q. when last tested: 112. A previous time tested: 107. In high school when tested: 121.

Born Mt. Vernon, Michigan. February 11, 1963. Dale Springs public schools. Dale Springs High School, class of 1981. Q__ P__ graduated forty-fourth in a class of one hundred eighteen. Did not win a scholarship to any college. Did not belong to any sports teams, school newspaper or yearbook etc. Highest grades in math except in senior year calculus where I fucked up.

I see my probation officer Mr. T__ alternate Thursdays 10 A.M., downtown Mt. Vernon. My therapist Dr. E__ Mondays 4 P.M., University Medical Center. Group therapy with Dr. B__ is Tuesdays 7 P.M.

I am not doing well, I think. Or maybe just O.K. I know they are writing reports. But I am not allowed to see. If one of these was a woman I would do better, I feel. They believe you, they are not always watching you. EYE CONTACT HAS BEEN MY DOWNFALL.

Mr. T__ asks questions like rolling off a tape. YES SIR I tell him NO SIR. I am employed. On a regular basis now. Dr. E__ is the one who prescribes the medication. Asks me questions to get me to talk. My tongue gets in the way of my talking. Dr. B__ throws out a question as he says to get the guys talking. They're bullshit masters. I admire them. I sit inside my clothes staring at my shoes. My whole body is a numb tongue.

I drive everywhere in my Ford van. It is a 1987 model, the color of wet sand. No longer new but reliable. It passes through your vision like passing through a solid wall invisible. My American flag decal big as a real flag in the rear window.

4

My bumper sticker is I BRAKE FOR ANIMALS. I thought it was a good idea to have a bumper sticker.

2

Is Time outside me, I started wondering in high school. When things began to go fast. Or is Time inside me.

If OUTSIDE you have to keep pace with fucking clocks & calendars. No slacking off. If INSIDE, you do what *you* want. Whatever. You create your own Time. Like breaking the hands off a clock like I did once so it's just the clock face there looking at you.

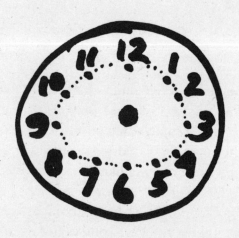

3

I am a registered part-time student at Dale County Technological College where I am enrolled in two three-credit courses for the spring semester. INTRO TO ENGINEERING & INTRO TO DIGITAL COMPUTER PROGRAMMING.

It was decided that Q__ P__ might become an ENGINEER. There are many kinds of ENGINEERING. Chemical ENGINEERING, civil ENGINEERING, electrical ENGINEERING, mechanical & aerospace ENGINEERING. The college catalog lists the requirements for majors. Q__ P__ might earn a degree in how many years Dad calculated.

In the detention center downtown where they locked me up awaiting Dad posting my bond I was observed doing rapid calculations in pencil. Up and down the margins of old magazines laying around. Weird: my hand moving like it had its own purpose. Like in eighth grade, algebra equations. Geometry problems except I didn't have a compass or ruler but drew the figures anyway. Long columns of numbers like ants just to add them up for the hell of it, I guess. I don't know why. This went on for a long time. For hours. I was sweating onto the magazine pages watching where the pencil point moved. Even after the pencil point got dull and the marks were invisible. Even when the guard was talking to me and I didn't hear.

They had me quarantined as they called it. Ninety-one percent of inmates at the detention center are black or Hispanic, white guys are put together in holding cells. I was with two white guys busted on drugs. I was tagged RACIAL OFFENSE. But it was not RACIAL. I don't know what RACIAL is.

I am not a RACIST. Don't know what the fuck a RACIST is.

Sweating & my hand holding the pencil was moving but I wasn't talking. Nor EYE CONTACT with anybody. It was observed how for that period of incarceration Q__ P__ was not talking & was not making EYE CONTACT with anybody.

In that way the fuckers slide down into your soul.

How Dad learned of these math calculations I don't know. Might have been they allowed him to observe me through one-way glass. On a surveillance camera. & the magazines were probably gathered & given to him for examination. He is Professor P__ & they call him so. He said the idea came to him then. To lend me tuition for the tech college where I would learn to be an ENGINEER. We would all forget about Mt. Vernon State U., that hadn't worked out. That was years ago.

A longer time ago when I was eighteen there was Eastern Michigan State at Ypsilanti. We had all forgotten about that long ago.

Quentin has a natural love of numbers Dad said to Mom. In my hearing. His voice thick like he was trying not to clear his throat of something clotted. *A gift for numbers. Inherited from me. I should have realized.*

THAT IS WHY I am a part-time student at Dale County Technological College. & I am studying hard. Dale Tech is seven miles from my current residence but no inconvenience for me, I told my probation officer Mr. T__, I have my Ford van I drive everywhere in. A distance of seven hundred miles is nothing, but I did not tell Mr. T__ that.

4

As of last Monday my residence is 118 North Church Street, Mt. Vernon. University Heights the area is called. Close by the big State University campus where Professor P__ teaches. (But Mom & Dad live in the suburb of Dale Springs, on the other side of town.)

At 118 North Church I am CARETAKER for this residence once my grandparents' home. None of the tenants know this fact I am certain and I would not be the one to tell them.

The property is still owned by my Grandma P__ who lives now in Dale Springs. But it is maintained by my father R__ P__ as a multi-tenant residence partitioned into nine rental units as approved by the zoning commission.

As a gesture of our trust, Quentin. Dad said.

Oh but Quentin will do a good job! We know that. Mom said.

Grandma's house is an old faded-red brick Victorian as they call it. With a smudged look in the front like somebody moved his thumb across it. Three storeys, plus the attic. An old addition at the rear used for storage. A big kitchen where tenants have "kitchen privileges" as they are called. A deep cellar which is OFF LIMITS to tenants. A stone foundation that is very solid. Clearing away some underbrush I discovered at the front right corner the date 1892 chiseled in the stone.

University students rent the rooms. The residence has been zoned for such a purpose since 1978 Dad was saying. If I knew this fact or not I don't know.

As CARETAKER of this property I live on the ground floor rear in the room provided for the CARETAKER. This is a room with its own bathroom, a shower stall & toilet. There have been previous CARETAKERS working for Dad but I don't know anything about them.

The back stairs to the upper floors & the stairs to the cellar are close by the CARETAKER's room which is convenient. Nobody can use these stairs except by passing my door. The CARETAKER's tools & equipment, work bench etc. are in the cellar.

I have access to all the floors of the house. Because I am CARETAKER. My father R__ P__ has entrusted me with this responsibility & I am grateful for the chance to make things up to him & Mom. My master key will open the door to any room in the house.

Most of the students who rent with us are foreign students. From India, China, Pakistan, Africa. Often they have trouble with their doors at first, so I am called upon to help. *Mr. P__* they call me. & I am always obliging though speaking no more than is necessary. & MAKING NO EYE CONTACT.

11

Thank you Mr. P__ they will say. Or *thank you sir*.

Their dusky skins & dark-bright eyes & dark hair that looks oiled. A smell of them like ripening plums. They are shy & more polite than American students & they pay their rent on time & don't notice things American students would notice & don't trash their rooms like American students which is why Dad says they are preferred tenants. Quiet in the evenings. At their desks studying. They all have contracts with a residence hall for meals so using the kitchen is kept to a minimum, I am mainly the one who uses the kitchen but I don't eat there I eat in my room watching TV. When I'm not out.

All the houses on North Church Street are big old brick or wood-frame Victorians. In big lots. In Grandma's & Grandpa's time when Dad was growing up here they were single-family residences of course. This was a classy neighborhood. University Heights. Grandma says it was after World War II the change began. In all of Mt. Vernon. Now North Church Street properties are rooming houses like ours or office buildings or taken over by the University like the house next door that is EAST ASIAN LANGUAGES. At the corner of North Church & Seventh three blocks away where the University president's house used to be the lot was razed for a high-rise parking lot. *So ugly!* Grandma says. Farther up is a Burger King just opened that Grandma has not seen yet where sometimes I get hamburgers & fries I bring back to my room to eat & watch TV or do my homework for my courses.

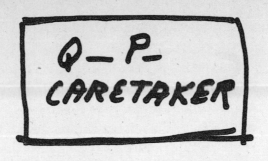

This is a small white card tacked beside my door.
I printed it myself with a black felt-tip pen.

5

Monday afternoons 4:00 P.M.–4:50 P.M. Mt. Vernon Medical Center. Dr. E__ asks *What are your dreams, Quen-tin. What are your fantasies.* Sit staring at the floor. Or at my hands I have scrubbed. There is a clock on Dr. E__'s desk that he can see & I can not. But I have my wristwatch *which was RAISINEYES'* which is an expensive digital watch. With an ebony face kept turned to the inside of my wrist where only I can watch the tiny numerals flashing bronze toward 4:50 P.M.

Trying to think of a dream to tell Dr. E__. To confide in Dr. E__. Something that might be a dream. Such as a person might have. Flying? In the sky? Swimming? In—Lake Michigan? In Manistee National Park in one of the unnamed deep & fast-flowing rivers? If only Dr. E__ would not stare at me. His power being that he is Dr. E__ a staff psychiatrist at the Medical Center. (Which is part of the State University.) Dr. E__ is my private therapist hired by Dad but he makes reports to the Michigan Probation Department & these are secret from me. I wish my head did not become heavy in Dr. E__'s office. It turns to a substance like pancake batter, very thick though soft, raw & pale.

Once in Dr. E__'s office when nobody had spoken for a while I felt my jaw drop like a dead man's & saliva trail across my chin. Slumped forward in the wooden chair with the hard slick bottom fitted to the cheeks of a wide ass. Head lolling & shoulders rounded & Dad was scolding whispering in disgust *Quentin for God's sake: you should see your posture.* A rasping sound like a wasp that might have been a snore.

There was embarrassment to it. Falling asleep in Dr. E__'s office. If that was what had happened. Dr. E__ glancing at the clock on his desk. Some papers on his desk.

Thinking his thoughts to type up on his computer after Q__ P__ leaves.

Is Dr. E__ a friend of Dad's I can't ask. I have reason to believe that this is so (both men are *senior professors* in the State University system) but both men would deny it if asked. I never ask.

After I leave his office Dr. E__ will pick up the phone & call Dr. P__ in his office at the University. *Your son Quentin is not making much progress I'm afraid. Did you know he never dreams. & his posture is so poor.*

That afternoon a few weeks ago Dr. E__ was too polite to notice that I had fallen asleep in the chair facing his desk. It was the strong medication maybe. He might think. Or maybe Dr. E__ did not notice. For he is sleepy sometimes, too. Heavy-lidded eyes like a turtle's. It was raining & water ran down the window behind his head in thin pissing streams.

Wrote my refill prescription & handed it to me, dosage as indicated. Dad's medical insurance covers it. Saying we can end our session a few minutes early this week (it is 4:36 P.M. by my watch) if that's O.K. with me, he had a staff meeting. It was O.K. with me.

6

Last night I was working late in the cellar. Emergency work repairing SEEPAGE DAMAGE in the old cistern. I am a hard worker if what I am doing has a purpose. I did not require sleep (did not take my nighttime medication) & so at 3 A.M. climbed to the attic where there is a star-shaped window at the front of the house. The peak of the ceiling is not high enough for me to stand upright & anyway I needed to crouch there looking up at the night sky where there was a MOON so bright it hurt my eyes! How I knew the MOON was there, from down in the cellar, I don't know. Shreds of cloud were being blown across the moon clotted & cobwebbed like thoughts moving too fast for you to hear.

So sad & squalid Quentin.

But now we are going to turn over a new leaf aren't we son.

You get to the attic by a steep narrow stairs at the rear of the third floor hallway. The attic is locked & OFF LIMITS to tenants like the cellar. I made my way silently in wool socks ot wishing to wake up the young Pakistani graduate student whose room is almost directly ben in the stairs.

Ramid would not   a safe specimen. Nor any of them beneath this roof. I never think of it.

In the attic there was a strong sharp smell of dust & that sweetish-sour smell of dead mice. I took a deep breath & another & another—my lungs like BALLOONS filling with air. Proof I don't need fucking medication. Am I sick? Who says? Shining my flashlight into the corners of the attic.

This could actually be for the best. Bringing a problem out into the open. The clarity of day.

Had I been here before? A long time ago a boy had climbed up here scared & in a hurry & he'd hidden something glittering & plastic on top of one of the beams back in the shadows but I don't know if I am supposed to be that boy or the other one bleeding & choking. But I was not wearing glasses then was I. (Did not begin wearing prescription lenses until aged twelve.) So it couldn't be Q__ P__. Or if I am confusing two times.

Fuck the PAST, it's NOT NOW. Nothing NOT NOW is real.

Quiet & not moving for many minutes. I have

trained myself to do so. & my eyes to penetrate the dark.

Shining the flashlight which is the CARETAKER's flashlight into the corners of the attic. Where shadows leap like bats. Smiling to see how, when light moves, light you hold in your hand, bright as starlight you make shadows leap. The shadows are there all along. BUT YOU MAKE THEM LEAP.

Crouched there at the window watching the MOON move out of sight. The way a dream will move & you can't stop it. Heart beating fast & hard. & beginning to feel horny. Excited, & blood seeping into my cock. I am not so safe in the attic as in the cellar where I have my work bench. I have moved my things to lock in the big drawer of the work bench with the CARETAKER's tools.

This space in the attic is like certain dreams I used to have where shapes meant to be solid start to melt. & there is no protection. & there is no control. Unlike the cellar which is safe UNDER GROUND, the attic is far ABOVE GROUND. The concentration of COSMIC RAYS is higher at higher elevations on Earth than at lower elevations.

The suggestion was made by Dad that I clean out the attic to reduce the *fire hazard* & I said O.K. I will begin that task soon. Right now the cellar is my Number One priority.

Now we are going to turn over a new leaf aren't we son & I said *Yes Dad.*

7

Of all of them, of Mom & Dad & Grandma & my sister Junie it has been hardest on Dad I know. For women, it is their nature to forgive. For men, it is harder.

Upsetting to Professor R__ P__ to learn certain things about his only son & these things a matter of public record. *How does your client plead*, the judge asked, & the lawyer Dad hired for me said, *Your Honor, my client pleads guilty.*

In my heart I did not plead GUILTY because I was NOT GUILTY & am not. But it was a RACIAL MATTER, too. The boy was black & Q__ P__ is white & the lawyer advised Dad this was a delicate issue in Mt. Vernon right now & the courts are carefully monitored, just be grateful we didn't draw a black judge.

But I am on good terms with the family again. This is a relief to all concerned. I have been driving Mom & Grandma to church & have attended four Sundays in a row. I have been driving Grandma to senior citizens' affairs & visiting friends. I have told them how sorry I am that I have hurt them. & how much it means to me that they trust me. *I will live up to your trust from now on* I told them.

The drinking is the cause of it & that will be terminated from now on.

It is fucking hard for me to hug them! Especially Dad. There is a stiffness in all our bones. But I do it & I believe I am doing it O.K. Mom & Grandma & Big Sis Junie were crying & there were tears leaking from my eyes I didn't wipe away.

When Judge L__ pronounced TWO YEARS there was a long moment when nobody spoke or breathed before he added SUSPENDED SENTENCE. Judge L__'s eyes which I had no choice (my lawyer so counseled me) but to look at reflected severity but also kindness.

Judge L__ is a fair man & not vindictive & not to be pushed around by special-interest groups it was said. He is known to Dad & Dad is known to Judge L__. I did not ask but Mt. Vernon is a place where important men in the professions know one another & it may be they belong to the same club or clubs. Dad has membership in the Mt. Vernon Athletic Club downtown not far from the courthouse.

Afterward Dad shook my hand so hard it hurt & did embrace me & there were tears in his eyes behind his glasses like his eyes were loose in their sockets like jelly about to slip out. Handed me the keys to his car so I could drive the family home.

KEY TO DAD'S CAR
(ACTUAL SIZE)

8

It has been hardest on Dad because R__ P__ is a name known to people. In Mt. Vernon where he & Mom have lived for thirty years & in Dad's profession where he is a distinguished man.

I don't mean that Dad is famous like Einstein or Oppenheimer or Dad's mentor at the Washington Institute Dr. M__ K__ are famous, or a great genius in his field but he is well known & admired & has many graduate students wishing to study with him. His Ph.D. is in both physics & philosophy or maybe he has two Ph.D.'s & they are both from Harvard unless one is from somewhere else, Dad was at a lot of other universities & knows a lot of people.

Before I was born when R__ P__ was a new Ph.D. he received a fellowship from the Washington Institute in D.C. & there he was befriended by the research scientist Dr. M__ K__ who won a Nobel Prize in 1958. In something like neurobiology, or cell biology. On the fireplace mantel of the house in Dale Springs where I grew up there is a photograph of men in evening dress & one of them is Dr. K — & one of them is Dad so young it's hard to know who he is & these two are shaking hands & smiling toward the camera. Pinpricks of red lights in their eyes from the camera's flash. Dr. K— is a balding white-haired old guy with a goatee like crotch hair and R__ P__ could be his son is what you'd think. Serious & intelligent & only twenty-nine years old but already he'd published some papers as he calls them. & already married to Mom (who is not in the photograph).

This photograph of Dr. M__ K__ & R__ P__ is to be found in three places: Dad's office in Erasmus Hall at the University & at the house in Dale Springs & in Grandma's house on a dining room wall with mostly family photos. Visitors stare at it and say *Oh! is that?*—& Dad says *Yes it is.* Blushing like a kid. *I didn't know him that well really—but he was a great man, he touched many lives & he certainly touched mine.*

When Dr. K__ died a few years ago at the age of eighty there were obituaries in *Time, People,* the *New York Times,* even the *Mt. Vernon Inquirer.* Dad clipped them all & had them laminated & they are on a wall in his University office. There was an obituary in the *Detroit Free Press* I saw & I should have torn it out & saved it for Dad but I forgot or it got lost. I was in Detroit where I go sometimes & stay in a hotel on Cass where I'm known as TODD CUTTLER a guy with curly red-brown hair & a moustache & he wears a leather necktie & looks kind of cool but also kind of a square, an asshole you could put something over onto if you tried. I was with Rooster & the two of us high & laughing leafing through the newspaper which always makes me laugh in the right mood & one of us was turning the pages fast & hard like a kid trying to rip them unless it was both of us & I saw this face on the obituary page NOBEL PRIZE LAUREATE DIES & I poked Rooster & said *This guy is somebody my Dad knows* & Rooster said *Yeah? No shit?*

9

It was five years ago the idea of creating a ZOMBIE for my own purposes first came to me in a brain storm to change my life.

Jesus! At such rare times you can feel the electrically charged neurons of the prefrontal brain realigning themselves like iron filings drawn by a magnet.

The Earth is continually bombarded by high-speed cosmic rays a voice was lecturing. An amplified voice. Was it Dad? Or somebody pretending to be Professor P__ with his nasal drone & habit of clearing his throat & pausing to let his words sink in.

Cosmic rays from outer space. Of an age many millions of years. More concentrated at higher elevations than lower. It was a darkened lecture amphitheater at the University. I did not know how I came to be there. I did not remember entering the amphitheater. It might have been observed that Q__ P__ had hidden himself purposefully to hear Professor P__ lecture, maybe he was seeking some knowledge or some secret? Like a dog seeking what dogs seek sniffing along the ground & their eyes alert. Except I must have nodded off in the back row &

when I woke up I did not know where I was at first which happened in those days when I was not so much in control of myself as I am now & going for as long as forty-eight hours unsleeping then crashing wherever I might be. My skin giving off a pulsing heat & my breath tasting of metal & seeing me people kept their distance from me not sitting in any row near. I was not living at home at the time but had a place downtown. It was hard to bathe there, no hot water.

Dad was at a podium to the right. A microphone around his neck. Two or three hundred students in the amphitheater taking notes & if Dad saw his son he gave no sign. But he could not see me I am sure in the darkness.

Quantifiable & unquantifiable material. Research into the early Universe suggests. On an illuminated screen at the front of the auditorium was a computer simulation as Professor P__ identified it of a section of the Universe two hundred million years ago. Demonstrating how the Universe evolved from its early smoothness & equitable distribution of matter to the present condition of superclusters & dark matter. *As much as ninety percent of the Universe's mass is in unquantifiable "black holes." Most of the Universe is therefore undetectable by our instruments & does not "obey" the laws of physics as we know them.*

There was a hum & a drone & vibrating in the room. That sense you have that the floor is tilting or the Earth shifting & settling beneath your feet. Professor R__ P__'s students were busy taking notes & I observed their bent heads & shoulders & it came to me that almost any one of them would be a suitable specimen for a ZOMBIE.

Except: you would want a healthy young person, male. Of a certain height, weight & body build etc. You would want somebody with "fight" & "vigor" in him. & well hung.

But the University students have been forbidden to me. After that ignorant incident that, lucky for Q__ P__, turned out O.K. It was dark behind the dorm & the kid was drunk & stooped over vomiting & gagging & when he looked up hearing me the tire iron slammed down over his ear crashing him to the ground before he could register seeing me so it was O.K. I was wearing my hooded canvas jacket & there were no witnesses, still I panicked & ran as I would never do now with more experience. But it was O.K. A lesson was learned.

& in Ypsilanti a long time ago so long I can't remember really I came to the same conclusion I think. For the fact is: any University student (with the exception of the foreign students who are so far from home) would be immediately missed. Their families care about them. & they have families.

A safer specimen for a ZOMBIE would be somebody from out of town. A hitch-hiker or a drifter or a junkie (if in good condition not skinny & strung out or sick with AIDS). Or from the black projects downtown. Somebody nobody gives a shit for. Somebody should never have been born.

Walked out of the amphitheater in the midst of the voice droning & went to the psych library to look up LOBOTOMY.

10

This is why: seeing the Universe like that (& that a replica of something billions of years extinct!) you see how fucking futile it is to believe that any galaxy matters let alone any star of any galaxy or any planet the size of not even a grain of sand in all that inky void. Let alone any continent or any nation or any state or any county or any city or any individual.

The idea came to me at that time too because I was having trouble keeping my dick hard with guys' AWAKE EYES observing me at intimate quarters.

11

I was living in a two-room place on Twelfth Street at Reardon, back in Mt. Vernon after spending some time in Detroit & this address was known to Dad & Mom & I was working at Ace Quality Box Co. (Dad thought as a clerk, in fact it was loading & unloading trucks) or maybe I'd just quit or been fired that time Dad dropped by. A few days after the lecture in the amphitheater I think. It was mixed up in my mind that Dad had seen me there in the dark HIS EYES PENETRATING THE DARK but maybe that was not so.

Aged twenty-seven & time to be ON MY OWN I told them. & I meant it.

(Except: Mom gave me $$$ when I was in need, not checks but cash. So Dad wouldn't know.)

The week following Thanksgiving 1988. BUNNY-GLOVES had been missing twelve days but there was never anything in the *Mt. Vernon Inquirer* or on local TV, why would there be? Set out from Detroit to Montana & not a trace.

How many hundreds, thousands in a single year. Like sparrows of the air they rise on their wings & soar & falter & fall & disappear & not a trace. & God is himself the DARK MATTER swallows them up.

Dale Springs pop. 8,000 is where the P__'s live & where their son Q__ grew up. A suburb of Mt. Vernon beside Lake Michigan & many tall trees & a meridian of green planted in geraniums in summer when you drive in crossing the (invisible) border from the City of Mt. Vernon. Six miles west & north of the University now a big sprawling campus. Downtown Mt. Vernon, this shitty neighborhood where I was renting my place is five miles to the south so go figure. Dad said he'd DROPPED BY to visit me.

The rapping at the door. My eyes flew open breaking the sticky lashes apart & my heart beat in a cold panic because NOW WAS NOT THE TIME.

Called out stammering & was up from the bed stumbling pulling on my trousers. Zipping up. Dragging the khaki blanket up over the mattress. The stained sheets, the sweet-stale smell. I was used to it by now & should have tried to open the window but didn't.

"O.K.," I said, "—I'm cool. O.K."

And it was Dad. My Dad. DROPPED BY to see how I was!

The chain latch was on the door. There was Professor R__ P__ smiling wearing his sand-colored corduroy face & his tweed asshole for his mouth & his black plastic-professor glasses riding the bridge of his nose. I fumbled opening the door. I tried to say the door wouldn't open any further, the latch was stuck. But DAD'S EYES a few inches away through the crack.

Out of a horny dream of BUNNYGLOVES, & fondling. His voice so clear in my head like it was before the change in it. & his eyes muddy-brown as KNOWING deepened in it & the pupils shrank to pinpricks.

"Quentin, hello! It's just me! Am I disturbing you?"

My hand moved & the chain latch was off. & Dad filled the doorway staring & breathless from the stairs. When R__ P__'s professor-goatee went from glossy brown to gray filings he shaved it off out of pride but there is the shadow of the goatee on his face still. That edge in his voice. "Son?"

The two of us the same height if I stood up straight which is hard & lifted my head to confront him. Asked how I was like always, & I said. & how was he, & things at home? & Mom & Grandma send their love. Yes & Junie. All wondering why I didn't call & didn't drop by & worrying (you know how women are!) maybe I'm sick. & DAD'S EYES darting as I had known they would fixing on the one thing. A pause & then asking, "That locker, that's new isn't it?" & a pause. &, "What's in that that requires a lock, son?"

I turned to see the five-foot metal locker leaning in the corner. Between the bed & the bathroom. Like I had not seen it before & was myself surprised.

"Just some gym things, Dad," I said. I said at once. "Jogging shoes, socks. Towels & stuff like that."

Dad asked, so reasonable, "But why does it require a lock?"

It was a combination lock like for a high school locker. I had memorized the combination & thrown the slip of paper away.

I was saying, "A lock came with it, Dad. From the Salvation Army. It was a real bargain at $12. It's a part of it. It's a way of getting the full use of the locker, I suppose."

"You wouldn't need to use it, though. Why would you?"

Distinguished Professor, Mt. Vernon State University. Dual appointments in Physics & Philosophy. Senior fellow of the Michigan State Institute for Advanced Research.

DAD'S EYES behind his shiny glasses. Looking at me like when I was two years old & squatting on the bathroom floor shitting & when I was five years old playing with my baby dick & when I was seven years old & my T-shirt splotched with another kid's nosebleed & when I was eleven home from the pool where my friend Barry drowned & most fierce DAD'S EYES when I was twelve years old that time Dad charged upstairs with the *Body Builder* magazines shaking in his hand. "Son? *Son?*"

"W-What?" I stammered. "I'm listening."

Dad was frowning. Fifty-seven years old with hairy black nostrils widening & pinching. "Why would 'gym things' require a special lock, son? Why would 'gym things' emit such a *smell?*"

It came to me: Dad thinks I am drinking again & taking drugs again, is that it? & indulging in unclean habits again risking my health?

Of BUNNYGLOVES what could Dad know? *Could* he know?

Between the bedsprings & the skinny mattress was the fish-gutting knife & the ice pick & the .38 nickel Smith & Wesson pistol but I was paralyzed & could not make a sudden move to protect myself. Staring at my hands which were trembling just slightly as if the building was vibrating from beneath. I did wonder, Could I strangle Dad? But he would resist, he would put up a struggle, and he is strong. & in a struggle we would be so *close*. I was staring at my hands as if I had never seen them before, like learning my name is Q__ P__ & that is who I am, & there is nobody else for me to be, the fingers were stubby like a kid's & the knuckles

34

scraped & the nails with queer milky half-moons uneven & broken & edged with grime. How many times I had scrubbed my hands with the gray soap from Ace & cleaned under the nails with a knifeblade & yet it had all come back.

& then the answer came to me.

I said, "—I bet I know what it is, Dad. A dead rat."

"A dead *rat*?"

"Or a mouse. Maybe mice."

"There are dead *mice* in here?"

Had he been thinking maybe food, spoiled food. Oh shit.

Rapping on the locker with his knuckles. The locker was painted army-green & badly scratched & wobbled when he struck it. Dad's corduroy face creased with disgust.

I said, "I k-know it's not the way I was brought up, Dad, or Junie. I'm sorry."

"Quentin, how long has it been like this in this room?"

"Not long, Dad. A day or two."

"Aren't you bothered by the smell yourself?"

"I'm going to do some cleaning this weekend, Dad."

"You've been sleeping right here beside this locker, this smell, & you're not bothered?"

"I am bothered, Dad. I just don't get uptight about it."

"It's very disturbing to me, son, that you might be lying to me."

"Well, I don't mean to lie, Dad. I just don't know what you're asking."

35

"I'm asking why this locker is padlocked, and why it smells. You know what I'm asking."

"Apart from the mice, Dad," I said, "—I don't know what you're asking."

"Your mother is worried about you, and I'm worried about you," Dad said, "—not just your future, but right now. What is your life right now, Quentin? How would you describe it?"

"My life 'right now'—?"

"Are you working at that box company?"

"Sure. Only today's a day off."

"What were you *doing* in here when I knocked on the door?"

"Taking a nap."

"A nap? At this time of day? With this—smell? Son, what has happened to you?"

I shook my head. I was looking at the floor but not seeing it.

If he looks in the bathroom, I thought, I'm fucked. The tub I didn't have time to scrub. The shower curtain so stained & speckled. BUNNY-GLOVES' underwear wadded and soaked with blood & the pubic hairs I'd scraped off on the floor.

"Son? I'm talking to you. How do you explain yourself?"

"Well," I said, "—apart from the mice, I don't see what's the problem."

It went on like that. DAD'S MOUTH shaped certain words emerging like balloons & my mouth shaped certain words & it was familiar to me & there was a comfort in that. For finally Dad gives up for *he does not want to know* & wipes his face with a handkerchief & says, "Quentin, the main reason I dropped by is—how would you like to come home with me for dinner tonight? Your mom has made banana custard pie," & I said, "Thanks, Dad, but I'm not hungry I guess. I've already eaten."

12

Twelve years old & in seventh grade & now I was wearing glasses & long-armed & skinny & hair sprouting under my arms & at my groin & their eyes sliding onto me & even the teachers & in gym class I refused to go through the shower refused to go naked moving through them & their cocks glistening & scratching their chests, bellies & some of them so muscular, so good-looking & laughing like apes not guessing except if seeing me & my eyes I couldn't keep still darting & swimming among them like minnows if seeing me they knew & their faces would harden with disgust QUEER QUEER QUENTIN'S QUEER & that time Dad charged upstairs to get me where I was doing homework in my room & yanked me by the arm & downstairs & into the garage & showed me the *Body Builder* magazines & the naked Ken-doll from the playground I'd brought back hidden behind stacks of old newspapers & he'd found his face splotched & furious & at that time Dad did wear a goatee like Dr. M__ K__'s & this too livid with outrage. Twisting the magazines in his hands like wringing a chicken's neck to spare himself the sight of the covers & the drawings somebody had done on them in fluorescent-red felt-pen ink. Nor the insides with more such drawings on center-fold models of male muscle bodies & the young guy who looked like Barry might've been in a few years & many pounds heavier & a shiny pink upright banana lifting from his groin & parts of certain photos scissored out. *This is sick Quentin* Dad's mouth worked, panted, *this is disgusting I never never want to see anything like this again in my life. We won't tell your mother* starting to say more but his voice gave out.

Together we burned the evidence. Back behind the garage where Mom would not see.

13

Frontal lobotomy, also known as leucotomy (from *leuco,* Greek for "white"). Most extreme and irreversible form of psychosurgery. Procedure destroys white matter in both the left and right frontal lobes of the human brain. Neuronal pathways connecting the frontal lobes with the limbic system and other parts of the brain are severed. Desired results: "flattening" of affect to reduce emotion, agitation, compulsive mental cognition and physical behavior in schizophrenics and other mental patients. Children as young as five may be so treated.

This page, I razored out of the textbook. Back behind the psych library stacks where nobody could see. I COULD ALMOST SEE MY *ZOMBIE* MATERIALIZING BEFORE MY EYES.

Another book even better, *Psychosurgery* (1942) by Dr. Walter Freeman and Dr. James W. Watts of George Washington University—

When the patient is unconscious I pinch the upper eyelid between thumb and finger and bring it

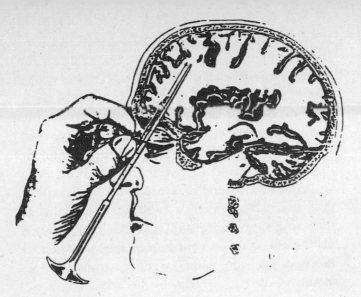

Figure 1. Transorbital lobotomy procedure. The leucotome, or "ice pick," is inserted with the aid of a mallet through the bony orbit above the eyeball. The handle of the leucotome is then rotated so that the cutting edge destroys fibers at the base of the frontal lobes.

well away from the eyeball. I then insert the point of the transorbital leucotome into the conjunctival sac, taking care not to touch the skin or lashes, and move the point around until it settles against the vault of the orbit. I then drop to one knee, beside the table, in order to aim the instrument parallel with the bony ridge of the nose, and slightly toward the midline. When the 5 cm. mark is reached, I pull the handle of the instrument as far laterally as the rim of the orbit will permit in order to sever fibers at the base of the frontal lobe. I then return the instrument halfway to its previous position and drive it farther to a depth of 7 cm. from the margin of the upper eyelid. Again I sight the instrument as carefully as possible, and take a profile photograph of it in this position. This is the nearest approach to precision of which the method can boast. Then comes the ticklish part. Arteries are within reach. Keeping the instrument in the frontal plane, I move it 15° to 20° medially and about 30° laterally, return it to the mid position, and withdraw by a twisting movement, at the same time exercising considerable pressure on the eyelid to prevent hemorrhaging. Then to the opposite side, using an identical instrument, freshly sterilized.

I was excited getting a HARD-ON razoring out these pages, I knew this was a TURNING POINT in my life. How many thousands of *transorbital lobotomies* these guys performed in the 1940s & 1950s & how easy to perform, the author of *Principles of Psychosurgery* stated he did as many as thirty sometimes in a single day using only a "humble" ice pick as he called it!

Dad & Mom had hoped for me to become a scientist like Dad, or a doctor. But things had not turned out that way. But I knew I could perform a *transorbital lobotomy* even if it was in secret. All I would need is an ice pick. & a specimen.

14

At Tuesday's group session Dr. B__ urged us to *speak from the heart.* There are eleven of us. Eyes are avoided. *O.K. men let's get the ball rolling, who wants to begin?* There was a weird buzz at the back of my head. Kept looking back over my shoulder & shifting my ass in the chair but there was nobody behind me or nobody I could see. *Remember nobody's judging anybody else. That's the bottom line, guys.*

Fluorescent lights & some of them flickering. Cement-block wall painted mustard yellow & posters & fliers & sign-up sheets & a picture of Magic Johnson with some message on it & no windows except the one door with thick glass reinforced with wires like circuits of the brain & I'm wondering if it's one-way glass & we are being observed like laboratory rats maybe videotaped? though when we came through that door that's the same door we come through every week I would swear.

O.K. men let's get the ball rolling, speak clearly & from the heart. Who wants to begin?

Bim goes first, Bim's a white guy my age with a face like crumbly cheese & the Haldol tremors & a perpetual runny nose so there's a glisten of snot in his nostrils like teardrops, once he gets talking & laughing & talking fast he can't stop & I'm staring at the floor trying to think what Q__ P__ can say, three weeks in a row sitting here staring at the floor & deaf-&-dumb like a moron. If you don't cooperate/communicate YOU'RE FUCKED. Next is this other white guy Perche in his forties always wears a plaid coat & necktie always grinning & try-ing to shake hands with everybody, saw me out on the street one day & called out QUEN-TIN! like we're buddies & I stood there staring at him not eye-contact but chest-level & he stares at me & comes a little closer his hand held out to shake & I'm in my own space rigid & not-breathing & finally he backs off saying *Excuse me, I thought you were somebody I know.* & next there's this fat guy, a kid younger than me with a beer gut all around his cowboy belt & pushing up toward his chin like a bloated frog, Frogsnout's my name for him & he talks too fast too & sweats & pants & though I'm not listening I can't help but hear, some bullshit about him *haunted by the memory of, can't stop thinking of, so fucking sorry for* his sister's kids he burnt up by accident pouring gaso-line around the house & lighting it for revenge not knowing anybody was home & this takes a long time. & there's the black guys of whom two are cool dudes I call Velvet Tongue & The Tease, these dudes true bullshit artists both on parole from

44

Jackson Q__ P__ could learn from but DON'T MAKE EYE CONTACT. So I don't.

Forgot my morning meds & lunchtime & so on the way down here swallowed two 'ludes. Eating a double cheeseburger & fries & drinking Bud in the van, got a six-pack at a 7-Eleven & drank four beers straight, throat's so fucking dry. Cruising the expressway & the riverfront & down by the projects. OFF LIMITS since sentencing. Taking a chance if a cop pulls me over & I'm drinking but no cop is going to pull me over, white guy with a neat haircut driving a van with O.K. head-lights, taillights, safe within the speed limit & keeping to the right-hand lane. Q__ P__ got his driver's license aged sixteen & always a damned careful driver.

So I'm cool & mellow & listening to the other guys or seeming so & Dr. B__'s frowning & nodding like they do, like they're listening, too & taking it all in. & I'm not going to panic 'cause it's my turn after the next guy. & I know I'm fucking up not *contributing to the discussion* as Dr. B__ calls it. & I know he's already been giving me bad marks or ??? on the reports. *Nobody's going to judge you, men. Just speak from the heart. It goes no further than this room, O.K.?*

My shoulders hunched like a vulture's & I'm staring at my shoes which are jogging shoes stained like rust. *Quen-tin? How about you?* & I open my mouth to speak & there's this voice comes out, it's Q__ P__'s but like another guy's too, somebody on TV maybe, or I'm imitating

45

Bim, Perche, Frogsnout, stammering saying how ashamed I was to betray the loving trust of my Mom & Dad & that was the worst part of what'd happened to me, not just this once but many times since the age of nineteen, though I had never been arrested before & never did anything *illegal* but many smaller things. (Why I said *nineteen* I don't know, just an age that sounded O.K. It was aged *eighteen* in fact, the incident at Ypsilanti & how upset Dad & Mom were.) I wished I could turn the clock back to infancy I said! & start Time again. When I was pure & good. When I was with God. I said I believed in God but did not think He believed in me because I was not worthy. There is that way Mom's face creases & collapses when she cries because she is getting old & my face collapsed like this & the guys were embarrassed & looked away except for Perche sucking it up like cum & Dr. B__ frowning & nodding. One of the black guys Velvet Tongue passed me a tissue but not looking at me & my voice was going fast now like a runaway trailer-truck down a mountain road. Said how sorry I was about the twelve-year-old boy I was accused of "molesting" (but did not supply details that he was *black* & *retarded* & a *natural zombie*—I'd thought!)—said I did not know what had happened exactly if I'd approached the boy myself in the alley back behind the dumpster where my van was parked or if the boy had followed me there & *picked me up* without my knowing. Because sometimes things happen to me I can't comprehend. Too fast &

46

confused for me to comprehend. This boy looking so much older than twelve with eyes piercing
like blades demanding money from me or he
would tell on me, he demanded $10 & when I
gave him $10 he demanded $20 & when I gave him
$20 he demanded $50 & when I gave him $50 he
demanded $100 which was when I lost it &
screamed at him & shook him BUT I DID NOT
HURT HIM I SWEAR.

By this time I was stammering & my face was
wet with tears! I had not known there were tears
inside my eye sockets so close to leaking & once
begun it's easy to cry & half the guys were looking
away from me & the other half mainly white guys
were looking & Dr. B__ was flush-faced like he'd
come in his pants asking questions about the boy
as if this was some kid I'd known like in the neighborhood not a total stranger & weird questions like
had I *felt affection* for the boy & did I feel that *feeling affection was being manipulated* & that was
why I *lost control*, it was *control of my own emotions* I had lost wasn't it? & feared? & I was shaking
now a little imitating Bim, the hand-tremors &
twitchy mouth & my face shining with tears & I
looked up at Dr. B__ for the first time daring to
make eye-contact because the tears protected me &
I said in a loud clear voice like it was a surprise to
me & a wonder—*Yes doctor. I felt affection & that
is why I lost control.*

After each of our sessions Dr. B__ fills out this
report for the probation office, I know. We are not

47

allowed to see these reports which are confidential but that evening I was told something to make me hopeful, Dr. B__ pulling at his beard like it's his dick & kindly smiling the way they do they're making a gift to you of your own shit. *Quen-tin you are making true progress at last, a breakthrough, getting in touch with your emotions Quen-tin!*

15

A true ZOMBIE would be mine forever. He would obey every command & whim. Saying "Yes, Master" & "No, Master." He would kneel before me lifting his eyes to me saying, "I love you, Master. There is no one but you, Master."

& so it would come to pass, & so it would be. For a true ZOMBIE could not say a thing that was *not*, only a thing that *was*. His eyes would be open & clear but there would be nothing inside them *seeing*. & nothing behind them *thinking*. Nothing *passing judgment*.

Like you who observe me (you think I don't know you are observing Q__ P__? making reports of Q__ P__? conferring with one another about Q__ P__?) & think your secret thoughts—ALWAYS & FOREVER PASSING JUDGMENT.

A ZOMBIE would pass no judgment. A ZOMBIE would say, "God bless you, Master." He would say, "You are good, Master. You are kind & merciful." He would say, "Fuck me in the ass, Master, until I bleed blue guts." He would beg for his food & he would beg for oxygen to breathe. He would beg to use the

49

toilet not to soil his clothes. He would be respectful at all times. He would never laugh or smirk or wrinkle his nose in disgust. He would lick with his tongue as bidden. He would suck with his mouth as bidden. He would spread the cheeks of his ass as bidden. He would cuddle like a teddy bear as bidden. He would rest his head on my shoulder like a baby. Or I would rest my head on his shoulder like a baby. We would eat pizza slices from each other's fingers. We would lie beneath the covers in my bed in the CARETAKER's room listening to the March wind & the bells of the Music College tower chiming & WE WOULD COUNT THE CHIMES UNTIL WE FELL ASLEEP AT EXACTLY THE SAME MOMENT.

16

Purchased my first ice pick, March 1988. Cruising
the van along Rt. 31 & out to the Lake Michigan
shore & through the little half-assed towns Stony
Lake, Sable Pt., Ludington, Portage & Arcadia. In my
down jacket, wool cap, my glasses with dark plastic
shades slipped over them, a week's growth of beard
& keeping my voice low like it's hoarse stopping at
a crossroads store selling groceries plus hardware &
it was no trouble making the purchase & nothing
suspicious. Old guy watching TV by a woodburn-
ing stove & he rings up my purchase on an old-
fashioned cash register & his face is wizened like a
prune & I say, making a joke, *A man needs a fucking ice pick this time of year, huh?—fucking winter,* & the old guy blinks at me like he doesn't know
the English language so I say, grinning & making a
joke of it, *These ice storms, huh?—fucking Michigan winter* & this time the old fart seems to hear or
at least sneers his lip & agrees. & I'm thinking
should he ever be asked to identify the purchaser of
said ice pick & they show him a photo of Q__ P__
(shaven, with regular glasses & no cap) he'll shake

his head & say *Naw, that don't look anything like him.*

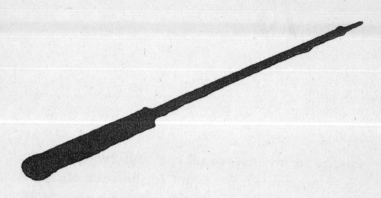

Parked the van overlooking the ice-jammed shore & the lake & the sky steely gray & a glare so you can't tell where one ends & the other begins so you could climb up from Earth into Heaven if you believe in that kind of shit WHICH Q__ P__ DOES NOT! & I had the ice pick in my hand poking & prodding & thrusting into its target & so EXCITED suddenly with no warning I COME IN MY PANTS before I can fucking unzip, oh Jesus IS THIS A SIGN WHAT'S TO COME?

17

Mondays & Thursdays are trash pick-up mornings on North Church. So I drag the yellow plastic cans out to the curb by 7:30 A.M. which is O.K. because I am an early riser not requiring sleep like weaker people. Wearing my sweats & a Tigers baseball cap & looking just ahead of me where I'm walking like I'm a guy minding my own business & there's this voice out of the fucking sky!—there's this soft humming voice!—& I almost didn't hear then I heard it & whirled around like it's Vietnam & I'm a hopped-up grunt like in the movies & it was one of the tenants!—just one of the tenants Ramid so polite on his way up to campus & hooded up like a little kid & with the face of a little kid & his eyes like chewy dates & he's asking do I need some help? & I'm staring at him, there's EYE CONTACT but only for a moment then I'm cool, I'm saying *no thanks it's my job. But thanks.*

18

Dr. E__ asks *What is the nature of your fantasies, Quentin?* & I am blank & silent blushing like in school when I could not answer a teacher's question nor even (everybody staring at me) comprehend it. Saying finally, so quiet Dr. E__ had to cup his hand to his ear to hear, *I guess I don't have any—what you call "fantasies," Doctor. I don't know.*

19

At the time of BUNNYGLOVES, RAISINEYES, BIG
GUY I did not have access to my caretaker's quarters
of course nor the cellar at 118 North Church. Only
my van & the two-room place on Twelfth Street. The
tub in the bathroom.

My procedures were crude & I was continually
thwarted in my experiments. A radio had to be
played loud, heavy-metal sound on WMWM out of
Muskegon & sometimes fucking ads would come on,
the intrusion of some stranger's voice at a delicate
moment. & if my hands shook or if I was 'luded-out
& could not perform as I bid my hands to do like in a
dream when you're moving through glue. & if I got
TOO EXCITED TOO FAST. Oh shit.

BUNNYGLOVES who I had such hope for, him being the first, convulsed like a madman when I
pushed the ice pick at the angle in the diagram
through the "bony orbit" above the eyeball (or whatever it was, splintering bone) & screamed through
the sponge I'd shoved & tied in his mouth actually
snapping the baling wire securing his ankles but he
did not regain consciousness dying in twelve min-

utes while I ran cold water on his face to wash away the blood & revive him. My first ZOMBIE—a grade of fucking F.

RAISINEYES lived for seven hours in the tub sometimes almost conscious & snoring or rattling his breath so I thought IT'S WORKING! IT'S WORKING! MY ZOMBIE! but I had to lift the eyelid of his remaining eye (I only "did" one) & secure it with tape, it never kept open by itself. I would move his arms & legs to get the circulation going. & handled & squeezed his cock (which remained limp & clammy-cool like a chicken's innards) but NOTHING HAPPENED. & then it was over & SHIT WHAT A DOWNER.

BIG GUY was most promising for by then I believe I had learned to use the ice pick skillfully, it's a skill you learn with practice, using a hammer like Dr. Freeman said instead of, what I'd been doing before, just pounding with the flat of my left hand, to drive the ice pick up into the "frontal lobe." Also, BIG GUY for a part-nigger part-Huron Indian drop-out college basketball player-junkie-dealer from Lansing was weird, he was so *healthy,* I mean looked *healthy,* his hair thick & glossy-black & his bones so long & hard, his muscles, flat stomach & chest hair & his penis a length of blood sausage, his skin a deep rich plum-black I was crazy to lick with my tongue & my teeth to gnaw. Even his toes, his big toes!—JUST CRAZY FOR HIM. Yet BIG GUY let me down like the others for he never regained what they call *consciousness* after the operation & like RAISINEYES was breathing these deep shuddering snoring gasps

56

after I yanked out the sponge thinking he was chok-ing on it. *Hey? Hey c'mon? You're O.K. c'mon open your eyes?* But the left eye I'd gone into with the ice pick was shot & the right eye wasn't much better, rolled back in his head like it wasn't even an eye but something else. BIG GUY lived maybe fifteen hours I think dying as I was fucking him in the ass (not in the tub, in my bed) to discipline him as a ZOMBIE & I only comprehended he was dead when during the night waking needing to take a piss I felt how cold he was, arms & legs where I'd slung them over me & his head on my shoulder to cuddle but BIG GUY was stiffening in rigor mortis so I panicked thinking I would be locked in his embrace!

My first three ZOMBIES—all F's.

Yet Q__ P__ did not give up hope. Nor have I to this day.

20

HOW A DUMB ACCIDENT CAN CHANGE YOUR LIFE.

Supposed to meet a guy, young Wayne State kid, at the fountain at Grand Circus Park, downtown Detroit, it was a hot muggy summer night seven, eight years ago & Q__ P__ in the city for the weekend alone & fresh-faced amid the winos around the pigeonshit fountain strung out on Thunderbird & heroin some of them so far gone you'd mistake a young guy for old, a white guy for black, eyes bloodshot or filmed over in mucus & skin gray-moldery like an exhumed corpse. & this was the time I think this was the time when I was taking a course in learning to be a real estate agent in Mt. Vernon, my big sis Junie's idea & it was a reasonable one, just didn't work out. Maybe I'd been drinking too but I wasn't drunk, for sure I am never what's called DRUNK but steady on my feet & steady-eyed, steely. & I was looking pretty damn good in my tight jeans & palomino-skin jacket worn for reasons of style despite the 90° heat, my hair like wings oiled & combed back from my face curving just under my ears. Just come from sleeping & waking dazed not knowing where I was at first in the balcony of one of the big old palatial movie theaters on Woodward FIERY BOY LOVE & FORBIDDEN ECSTASIES & now it was midnight & thrumming from electricity though Woodward & Gratiot were practically deserted. & I waited for my friend, & waited, & he never came & I was pissed wasting much of a Saturday night & went to some bars on Grand River & must've gotten drunk & afterward walking along the sidewalk I was grabbed from behind by two or three unknown assailants, might've been more of them standing watching, a nigger gang?—just teenagers but big & strong & laughing-elated doped to the eyeballs throwing me down like it's a football tackle onto the filthy pavement & KICK KICK KICKING yelling *Where's your wallet, man? Where's that wallet?* I'd just seen a cop-cruiser pass through the intersection but nobody came to my rescue, if there were witnesses on the street they didn't give a shit just walked away, or stood laughing at whitey getting pounded, his glasses broken & nose bloodied & the more he squirmed like a fish on a hook the more the kids laughed & yelled ripping my palomino-hide jacket & got my wallet within seconds but still laughing, chanting *Where's your wallet, man? Where's that wallet?* like these were words to some nigger music which maybe they were. & I'm sobbing & trying to say *No! don't hurt! oh hey please! no, NO!* like not even a child but a baby, an infant might, & I'm pissing my pants & when it's over & they're running away I don't even know it I'm still sobbing, trying to hide my face, double up like a thick writhing worm trying to protect my insides with my knees, & a long time afterward somebody comes over to peer at me & ask, *Man, you alive? You want some ambulance or somethin'?*

It was when I saw my face next day the revelation came.

Blinking & leaning close to the mirror because I didn't have my glasses, & there was this FACE! this fantastic FACE! battered & bandaged (& blood leaking through already) & stitched (more than twenty stitches they gave me at Detroit General for three bad gashes) & the lips bruised & swollen & these were bloodshot-blackened EYES UNKNOWN TO ME.

& I understood then that I could habit a FACE NOT KNOWN. Not known ANYWHERE IN THE WORLD. I could move in the world LIKE ANOTHER PERSON. I could arouse PITY, TRUST, SYMPATHY, WONDERMENT & AWE with such a face. I could EAT YOUR HEART & asshole you'd never know it.

21

Phone rang & it was Mom. Asked how I was & I said. Asked about my classes at Dale Tech & I said. Asked about my sinuses & I said. Asked about the care- taker's job (which was Dad's idea for Q__ P__, not Mom's) & I said.

Has it been six months since my dental check-up Mom asked & I said I didn't know & Mom said she was afraid it was more than six months possibly a year? & did I remember all the dental work I'd had to have done ten years ago when I'd neglected to have my teeth examined regularly & cleaned & I said & Mom said should she make an appointment for me? with Dr. Fish? & I stood there holding the phone re- ceiver & through the opened doorway & along the hall at the mailboxes there was the one called Akhil talking with the one called Abdellah & I wondered what they were saying. If I could hear them, if the language they spoke was my own.

22

Couldn't remember where I'd hidden them. Groping around on top of the beams filthy with cobwebs & desiccated husks of insects & my fingers came away empty. ROUND-LENSED GLASSES & CLEAR PLASTIC FRAMES. In school across the aisle his silky hair & face I stared at & the light winking off the lenses like there was a SECRET CONNECTION between us.

Except there wasn't.

Or maybe there was & he denied it. Pushing me away if I stood too close in cafeteria line. Bruce & his friends & I'd slip in behind them & pretend like I was standing with them sometimes pushing up against them, a boy's back.

BRUCE BRUUCE BRUUUUCE! I would whisper jamming my fingers in my mouth & my mouth against the pillow wet from drooling.

A door opened in my dream & I *was* BRUCE.

His parents came over to talk to Dad & Mom. I hid away hearing their terrible voices. Dad came finally to get me—*Quentin! Quen-tin!*—flush-faced & his glasses damp against his nose & his goatee quivering when he discovered me hiding curled up like a big slug behind the trash pail in the cupboard beneath the sink. *What do you mean hiding from me, son? Do you think you can hide from* me*?* Led me by the arm into the living room where Mom was sitting stiff-smiling on the cream-colored brocaded sofa with two strangers, a man & a woman, Bruce's parents, & their eyes like shattered glass in their angry faces & Dad stood with his hands lowered to my shoulders & asked in a calm voice like somebody on TV news had I *purposefully* hurt Bruce? tangling his neck & head in the swing chains *purposefully*? & I jammed my fingers in my mouth, I was a shy slow-seeming child & wide-eyed & the light of fear always quick in my face. I stared at the carpet & the little round plastic things that bore the weight of the coffee table & the sofa & were intended to protect the carpet & I wondered if there was a name for such things & who is the source of NAMING, why we are who we are & come into the world that way—one of us BRUCE, & one of us QUENTIN. Mom began to speak in her high quick voice & Dad cut her off calmly saying it was my responsibility to speak, I was seven years old which is the age of reason. & I started then to cry. I told them no it was Bruce, it was Bruce who hurt me, scared me saying he would strangle me in the swing chains because I wouldn't touch his thing but I got away, I got away & ran home & I was crying hard, my elbows & knees were scraped & my clothes soiled.

& Mom hugged me, & I was stiff not wanting to press into her breasts or belly or the soft place between her legs.

& Dad said it was all right, I was excused. & Bruce's parents were on their feet still angry but their power was gone. Bruce's father called after me like a boy jeering, *& what did you do with our son's glasses?*

23

Mom called. Left a message on the answering tape saying she'd made an appointment for me with Dr. Fish. Also would I like to come to dinner Sunday.

At the time the phone rang I was on the third floor in Akhil's room using a screwdriver to open the rusted furnace vent which had been only partway open. Crouched over & my face heavy with blood. Akhil is from Calcutta, India. Maybe he is Hindu? A physics grad student & maybe one of Dad's but I would never inquire nor would Akhil make any connection between the CARETAKER of this property in his jeans & sweatshirt & PROFESSOR R__ P__ who is so distinguished.

Akhil is shy & dusty-skinned & slender as a girl. In his mid-twenties at least but looks fifteen. Their blood so different from ours. Ancient civilization. Monkey-like. He speaks English so soft & whispery I almost can't hear—*Thank you sir*. Take care NOT TO MAKE EYE CONTACT but in our mutual awkwardness I did glance at him, & he was looking at me, he was smiling. Eyes liquidy-brown like a monkey's would be, a warm glisten in them.

Oh Jesus my eyes slid down him, the slippery length of him. Melting at his crotch. A shimmering puddle at his feet.

Q__ P__ was observed standing quickly. Had to get out of that room. My voice loud & American & movements clumsy but I believe this is what any CARETAKER of any rooming house in University Heights would say under the circumstances *That's O.K., it's my job.*

24

Thursday was Q__ P__'s busy day!

Chores at the house. Drive-in breakfast in the van at Wendy's on Newaygo Street. Swallowed two uppers with black coffee. Swung around to Third Street to XXX VIDEO to return last night's video & rent another, a new release. Feeling O.K. 10 A.M. meeting with Mr. T__ in the county services building, the old wing beside the courthouse. Where you walk through the metal detector & two county sheriff's deputies give you the eye. & upstairs in the probation dept. Mr. T__'s door is shut & I wait for a few minutes & I'm O.K., I'm cool. Shaved last night & had a shower yesterday morning, or day before. Always wear a necktie, coat & a belt for my trousers at Mr. T__'s. A black dude looking like Velvet Tongue waiting for his probation officer too but I don't want to look too close nor does he. & Mr. T__ calls me in & there is a handshake & *Have a seat, Quentin, how're things going?* & I say. *How's your caretaking job?* & I say. *How's your classes at Dale Tech?* & I say—pretty good, a B in Intro to Computer & a B− in Intro to Engineering & Mr. T__

67

nods & writes something down. Or anyway doesn't question.

Asks me how's my group therapy, am I attending faithfully & I say. How's my private therapist & I say.

& my medication? still taking your medication? & I say.

Tells me his sister's son got a degree in electrical engineering from Dale Tech & has a good entry-level job with GE in Lansing.

Tells me our next meeting he's sorry he's going to be away on vacation so we'll schedule it for four weeks same time same place O.K.?

There is a handshake at the end of the session. & Q__ P__ observed polite & respectful YES SIR. NO SIR. GOODBYE SIR.

Leaving Mr. T__'s office I see the black dude so resembling Velvet Tongue is just leaving his probation officer too & I hold back letting him get to the elevator first & take it down without me.

NO EYE CONTACT ANYWHERE BENEATH THIS ROOF.

Then out to Dr. Fish in Dale Springs. Driving the expressway north & out of the city. The edge of the lake. Tin-colored & the sky the same color. 11:30 A.M. appointment, same office in the same building Dr. Fish has had for years. Receptionist is new & doesn't know me nor the female assistant, Asian-American with a flat face & breathy voice, calls me in & puts on her gauze mask & rubber gloves & seats me in the chair & prepares me for X-rays & teeth cleaning & I'm a little stiff & she lowers the chair with a pneumatic hiss & my stomach lurches & eyes shoot open & the girl is looking at me *Sorry! was that too fast?* For just that instant I was BIG GUY going under, or RAISINEYES, or who was it—BUNNYGLOVES. & I saw Velvet Tongue in my place in my own body in this chair & it's like my eyes were his! But it passes. I'm O.K. The girl lays the lead bib over my chest to protect me from X-rays & arranges the little X-ray cardboards in my mouth so I'm almost gagging but I hold on, I'm cool. The girl says *Please hold, don't move* & noiseless leaves the room & sets the machine humming. It might be that Q__ P__ is being photographed and/or videotaped here, might be Q__ P__'s actual brain is being X-rayed & the negatives sent to the county offices & East Lansing, the capital of Michigan & the F.B.I. in D.C. & to Dad c/o Physics Dept., Mt. Vernon State University. But I am not agitated, I am calm & unsuspecting. I have nothing to hide. What happened with the black boy was Q__ P__'s first offense, & a suspended sentence followed no actual jail time beyond the detention center—THAT IS THE PUBLIC RECORD. Flatface in her gauze mask returns & I'm almost asleep so calm & she takes out the X-ray cardboard & positions another & leaves the room again & sets the machine humming. & again. & again. WHEN Q__ P__ FIRST REALIZED THAT EVERYTHING HAPPENS AGAIN & AGAIN. & SOME PEOPLE KNOW, & SOME PEOPLE NEVER KNOW. Seventh grade, when my friend Barry died. When I PEELED OFF THE CLOCK HANDS. Flatface returns & the next step is cleaning my teeth & flossing which takes a long time. At a distance there is prickling & stinging in somebody's mouth but I'm almost asleep. *Please rinse,* & I wake up rinsing my mouth taking care to shut my eyes not wanting to see the blood-tinged liquid. Somebody's gums smarting & bleeding. This goes on for a while & finally it's over & Dr. Fish himself comes in & he's wearing a gauze mask too & rubber gloves & I feel a little shiver, excitement like a spike in the cock, behind the mask & glasses you don't know Dr. Fish is an old guy in his fifties at least, his hair's still O.K. unless it's dyed?—& he's looking at the teeth chart the female assistant has handed him & the X-rays & asking me how I am, how's the family Quentin, & the high school, he's confusing me with my sister Junie but that's O.K. Now Dr. Fish examines my mouth & he's fast & frowning & up close you can see the turtle-pouches around his eyes. This the man to see into your soul. *Please rinse Quen-tin.* Laying down one of the silver picks on a tray on a wad of cotton batting, the tip is shining with blood. There's a sick excited sensation in my gut, I'm rinsing my mouth & can't stop myself from seeing tendrils of blood in the water, I'm faint & excited & wish I could see Dr. Fish's hands & that silver pick in Q__ P__'s mouth like on a video! *Sorry if this hurts, Quen-tin,* Dr. Fish says, it's his mouth saying it, another pick in his hand, *you haven't been in for an exam in quite a while, eh?—almost three years. Afraid you've got several cavities &*

70

what might be the start of pyorrhea. Then the exam is over & Dr. Fish removes his gauze mask & rubber gloves & he's smiling asking do I have any questions? any questions? & he's ready to move on to the next patient in the next examining room & I'm clumsy-shaky rising from the chair & Dr. Fish is looking at me & I can't think of any question to ask him & he's turning to leave & I think of one.

"Do bones float?"

"Excuse me?"

"Bones. Do bones float?"

Dr. Fish stares at me & blinks once, twice. "What kind of bones?—human, or animal?"

"There's a difference?"

"Well, there might be." Dr. Fish shrugs & frowns backing off, I get the idea he's stalling not knowing the answer. "It would depend, too, on whether the bones were heavy, or, you know, dried out—hollow & light. If so they would float, I'm sure." There's a pause & he adds, "You mean float in water?" & I nod sort of vague & he's at the door, a little wave of his hand like a Thalidomide flipper, "Well, Quen-tin. See you next week?"

It was already arranged that the bill would be sent to Mom. No need for me to stop at the front desk. The receptionist called out surprised asking did I wish to make an appointment? & I mumbled no, I'd call sometime. & out of there, & that smell, fast. & in the van able to breathe & driving back to Church Street it came to me Fuckface Fish didn't know the first fucking thing about BONES. Dentists are not

79

doctors. Nor scientists of any kind. Probably didn't know any more than Q__ P__.

A MEMENTO of the visit, though, in my pocket.

25

FUCKING SORRY to be missing so many classes at Dale Tech. I don't know how it happens. Especially since I am determined to *turn over a new leaf* this time.

Except in Intro to Engineering I fucked up the first quiz, got a score of 34 ("F"). & missed the second. & when I got to the computer lab to do my assignments I'm behind in, there was a weird suspicious smell like formaldehyde that might've been a trick. (For the part of BIG GUY I'd saved, two-three years ago, I'd needed at least a quart of formaldehyde & got some from a biology lab at Mt. Vernon pretending I was a student, in my stick-on goatee & heavy glasses & carrying a briefcase I can pass for a grad student anywhere.) & the instructor is a young guy who looks right through me like there's a blank space where I am.

Dad has paid my tuition & I have insisted I will pay him back out of my caretaker's wages, as soon as things get settled. I still owe on my van & there are other expenses. Mom says I am careless with money spending on friends & making loans that will

73

never be repaid, I'm like her with a *generous heart* she says & not many *money-management skills.* Since the trouble last year—the arrest & the hearing & the suspended sentence etc.—Dad looks at me differently I think, I'm not 100% sure because I am shy to raise my eyes to his but I think it's like he is fearful of me as in the past he was impatient & always finding fault. Like Q__ his only son was a student failing a course of his. Yet I believe he is thinking we are all pretty lucky like my lawyer said. No matter the shame to the P__ family that Q__ is an *"admitted" sex offender* at least Q__ is not incarcerated at Jackson State Prison. At least his twelve-year-old "victim" was not injured. Or worse. Dad saying again & again *Think of it as an investment in our joint future, son! You can pay me back when you're able.* His jaw like he's got lockjaw but he's smiling with that wrinkly little pink-asshole mouth & his professor eyes watery inside his glasses.

Mom hugs me & stands on tiptoe to kiss my cheek. Her bones are like dried sticks I could break in my hands so I stand very straight & still not breathing to inhale her smell. What that smell is I do not know & do not name. Mom was a plump woman once with soft big breasts like balloons filled with warm liquid unless I am remembering her wrong. Dr. E__ says all mothers are big in memory because we were tiny infants nursing at the breast. Dr. E__ says there is the GOOD BREAST & the BAD BREAST. There is the GOOD MOTHER & the BAD MOTHER. *You know we love you Quentin* Mom says like a tape when a button is punched *This time things will turn out well.*

I say, *That's right, Mom.*

I say, *I'm sure going to see to that, Mom.*

These past ten months or so I've been driving out to Dale Springs & taking Mom & Grandma to church, & I'm missing some Sundays now but I intend to get back on schedule soon. Mom says *This time things will turn out well. With God's will.* & Grandma says, *This time things will turn out well. With God's will Amen.*

26

EXCEPT: the old dreams starting again in this new bed in this very house I'd visited so much as a little boy, Junie & me the grandchildren Grandma & Grandpa loved. They never knew Q__ P__ but they said they loved him. These old dreams now I've stopped taking my medication, I'm waking with a HARD-ON big as a ROCKET & sizzling-exploding going off LIKE A COMET'S TAIL. My cum is thick & clotted & gluey-hot wiped on the bedsheets, on the curtains, on the cardboard pizza box & napkins from *Enzio's* I folded to an inch square & placed in Akhil's bed (which was not that neatly made, not what you might expect) one afternoon when the house was empty.

Waking up in my caretaker bed at the ground floor rear of 118 North Church Street & I'm shuddering-groaning as the ORGASM slams through me like a bolt of electricity. Dreaming I'm strapped in the dentist's chair & lowered helpless & knives & picks in my mouth till I'm choking with my own blood. I'm feeling O.K. once I get up & turn the TV to "Good Morning America" & I boil some black coffee & take some uppers I pick up on the street when required.

& I remember the computer class was the day before. Or I'm driving out to Dale Tech & it's the wrong day, or the wrong time of the right day. Because Time is like a tapeworm jammed inside you in any direction. So I drive out anyway once the van is IN MOTION headed in that direction I'm superstitious about changing course just on impulse.

& if there's a hitch-hiker along the route, often just off the expressway I'll probably stop & give him a ride & I will observe him detached as a scientist calculating what kind of ZOMBIE he might make. But I am never tempted so close to home. & out at Dale Tech which is this crappy fifth-rate place everybody at the University including Professor R__ P__ looks down their asses at I will park my van in lot C I have a sticker for & cross "campus" (just concrete & scrubby strips of grass & stick-trees half of them dead over the winter) thinking *O.K.! I'll visit my profs* to explain there's an illness in the family, my Mom in a struggle with cancer, or Dad with a bad heart but I can't find their offices or if I find the office it's in the wrong building or the wrong wing of the right building & by the time I get to the right office it's shut, door's locked, the cocksucker is gone for the day. Or say I get sidetracked trailing some young guys from my engineering class into the student union where I'll have cups of black coffee till my eyeballs spin like pinwheels sitting seeing who's around ANYBODY KNOW ME? ANYBODY WANT TO SIT WITH ME? squinting seeing if I recognize anybody, if it's O.K. to sit with some of them, maybe they're in my engineering class or maybe computer or I look enough like somebody they know so it's O.K. I'm carrying some textbooks, it looks like, & my hair cut & not in a pony-tail or straggling down my shoulders since the arrest though I am wearing RAISINEYES' funky leather slouch-brim hat & BUNNYGLOVES' soft-bunny-fur-lined leather gloves are in the pocket of my $300 sheepskin jacket & my aviator-style amber prescription lenses are in BIG GUY's frames so I look pretty fucking cool I think for a shy white guy on the downside of thirty, weak chin & hairline receding. & it's weird how friendly the Tech students are, & how trusting. Like if you are enrolled & a student you are one of them & no questions asked. All of them commuters like me living in Mt. Vernon or the county & most with part-time jobs or even full-time, like me. Even sometimes a girl will pull out a chair to sit at my table if she knows some-body with me. *Hi!* she'll say like a high school cheer-leader. Like the girls at Dale Springs High who looked through Q__ P__ those years like he didn't exist. *Are you in my computer class?—you look familiar.*

I should mention my handtooled kidskin boots just a little too big for me courtesy of Rooster. Last observed striding along the street in Greektown, De-troit, Thanksgiving weekend 1991.

Never have selected any specimen except the black boy I don't count, from the Roosevelt projects, from Mt. Vernon & vicinity. But it is a shrewd idea to keep in practice speaking with them. Though mainly I listen. To learn their words, their slang. *Like* they say, *cool* they say, *that's cool!* every few words. *Gross, fucked-up, weird, wasted, retro, wild, far-out bummed*—the words don't change that much, & there are not many of them. It's more the way they move their hands, mouths, eyes. Though shrinking from their eyes unless I'm wearing my dark plastic shades.

Sometimes like Mom says I'm too generous paying for somebody's lunch or beers or whatever. Or actually lending money. & driving one or two of them home sometimes if they've missed their bus going a few miles out of my way into suburbs not-known to me & *No trouble!* I say & in such instances Q P 's kindness will be remembered, my face & the Ford van with the AMERICAN FLAG decal on the rear window. A big decal exactly fitting the rear window. If I needed a character witness (for instance at a trial) you would remember Q__ P__ from Dale Tech & the fact that I was kind.

Once lent a skinny Chinese kid my sheepskin jacket on a freezing winter night, no questions asked. & he returned it, maybe two weeks later but he returned it. Engineering student named "Chou" or "Chih" with a *ping!* sound in it. & his eyes shining-black & he did not seem so young & so innocent as most of them but when he said *Thanks, man* all I said was a mumble *Sure.*

79

27

That last time in my place on Reardon St. I was taking a chance bringing NO-NAME home. Picked him up on I-96, Grand Rapids exit ramp but he said he was from Toledo & traveling west. Fighting the drug eyes rolling sideways in his head like marbles. *Hey man I guess I don't want to do this O.K.?—lemme go man* & I told him I wanted him to stay with me like we were friends, brothers, I told him I would pay him well & he wouldn't be disappointed & he was sweating saying *Man I'm cool won't tell anybody I swear just lemme out of here man please?— O.K.?* & I tightened the cord so his big eyes bulged & his skin was ashy-plum & the lips I could not take my eyes off were ashy & it was shooting through me like electricity HE KNOWS! NOW HE KNOWS! NO TURNING BACK! which is the point that must be reached. The threshold of the black hole that sucks you in. A fraction of a second before & you are still free but a fraction of a second later & you are sucked into the black hole & are lost. & my dick hard as a club. & big as a club. & the sparks of my eyes. & I did not stammer as when first he swung into the van this cool dude eyeing whitey & his easy smile like *Here I am, man, what're you going to do about it?* In the back the old battered *Elements of Geophysics* textbook to provide a false clue, & my stick-on woolly moustache & hair parted weird-neat high on the left side of my head & in the tavern in Grand Rapids where we had a few beers he did the talking & I sat quiet just listening & if anybody saw us it was NO-NAME they saw & some white guy who never was there.

Then home with me & the promise of a hot bath, home-cooked meal vodka & clean sheets etc. NO-NAME grinning thinking he'd be sucked off by whitey & paid for his trouble & maybe clear out whitey's possessions but that was not how it came about & the panic in his eyes said this was so. I said, *I am not a sadist, I am not a torturer, I think you are terrific, I ask you to cooperate & you will not be hurt.* I was excited, I had to unzip. He saw, & he knew. You know even when you don't. It was two barbiturates I gave him mashed & in vodka. But they were slow to take effect & he was struggling & I said how many times *I will not hurt you* I said *if you lay still.* But his struggling made things worse for him & he didn't cooperate. He was crying, I saw he was just a kid. Maybe nineteen years old & he'd acted so much older, so cool! Jammed the kitchen sponge into his mouth seeing the flash of a gold tooth. He was near to choking so I had to be careful, I did not want to lose him. He was tied securely for his own safety, he was drugged & should have been anesthetized by now but it was taking too long. The way the doctors did lobotomies was to zap their patients first with electric shocks to render them unconscious but I didn't have the nerve I feared I would electrocute NO-NAME & myself both. He was in the tub now naked & the water was running & that freaked him HE KNOWS! HE KNOWS! though he could not see the ice pick yet. Snaky-supple kid with that gold tooth—a real TURN-ON. Reddish-kinky hair & a deep red sheen to his skin. Like oxblood shoe polish, Dad's shoe polish I remember from years ago at home. Good-looking in fact FABULOUS-LOOKING & they know it but it's too late once Q__ P__ takes over. I secured his head in the clamp & now brought the ice pick (which I had sterilized on the hot-plate burner) to his right eye as indicated in Dr. Freeman's diagram but when I inserted it through the "bony orbit" NO-NAME freaked out struggling & screaming through the sponge & there was a gush of blood & I came, I lost control & I came, so hard I kept COMING & COMING LIKE A CONVULSION I couldn't stop nor even breathe I was groaning & gasping for air & when it was over & I was in control again I saw the damage done—fucking ice pick rammed up to the hilt in NO-NAME's eye up into his brain & the black kid was dying, he was dead, blood gushing like from a giant nosebleed, another fuck-up & NO ZOMBIE.

28

& then the disposal of. The heavy weight of.

SO HEAVY. Like they're doing it on purpose, RE-SISTING.

Wrapped naked in green garbage-pail liners & tied with rope & on the outside wrapped in canvas & tied with baling wire. Dragged by night by stealth & infinite care. Down the stairs & into the van, the rear of the van carefully prepared for its cargo. SO HEAVY! Q__ P__ sweating in even cold weather. Lifting weights & working out at a gym like I do from time to time & mean to do on a regular basis as every therapist I've ever had recommends hasn't built up the muscles I would wish in the upper body & thighs.

The disposal of, these FABULOUS-LOOKING guys, it's a DOWNER.

Leaves me depressed if I'm not careful, back on my regimen of medication. & the fucking medication has side-effects so they get you both ways.

Q__ P__ always drives at the speed limit & obeys all traffic regulations. Whether there is *contraband cargo* aboard the van or not. Sometimes impatient drivers sound their horns at him moving slow & cautious (for instance in rainy weather, in snow) in the right-hand lane. But no response. No lowering the window & yelling out or waving the .38 pistol & firing into somebody's surprised face LIKE THEY DO IN DETROIT, MAN!

A landfill or dump is most strategic of course where the ground is already broken. & far from home base—seventy, one hundred, two hundred miles is Q__ P__'s rule. The extra effort is worth it like purchasing a new moustache, wig or whiskers every time. Vacant lots, wooded areas near parks— risky because kids play in them, & dogs. Dogs are your natural enemy if you don't dig deep. But empty marsh land beyond the Interstate in some lonely place where nobody goes is a good bet & weighted down with a tire iron & baling wire dropped into deep water—NO-NAME was dropped into a river in Manistee National Forest east of Crystal Valley.

& never a ripple, nor any word. Never a news item. No obituary. He did in fact have a name but it did not suit him.

Only this single memento I have of him in my carekeeping: one of Q__ P__'s most prized good-luck charms.

 GOLD TOOTH (ACTUAL SIZE)

How many times. I keep mementos but no records. My clock face has no hands & Q__ P__ has never been one to have hang-ups over personalities or the past, THE PAST *IS* PAST & you learn to move on. I could be a REBORN CHRISTIAN is what I sometimes think, & maybe I am waiting for that call.

In the meantime I have the basement of my grandparents' old house entrusted to me as CARETAKER.

29

A little sickness in the air from so much fragrance everywhere—

somebody's left-behind *New Anthology of English Verse* & I leafed through it in the student union, not at the tech college but at the University where sometimes I come by in the early evening & these words from a poem by "Gerald Manley Hopkins" leapt out at me & rang like the bell of the Music College.

Because now it is spring, it is April & Q__ P__'s first year of probation is behind him.

30

Dad & Mom & the relatives were ashamed but THAT
IS HOW IT PLAYS OUT as my lawyer, in fact he is
Dad's lawyer, in Dad's hire, has said. THAT IS HOW
IT PLAYS OUT.

If your son had come up before a black judge, or a
woman judge—it might've been much, much worse.

Q__ P__ was allowed after negotiation (in which
Q__ P__ took no part) to plead guilty to *sexual misdemeanor committed against a minor.* My lawyer
& the prosecution lawyer worked it out. & Judge L__
was understanding. People were saying where
money changes hands & it is the word of an inexpe-
rienced white man, unmarried, thirty years old,
against the charge of a black boy from the projects,
& this black boy, twelve years old, from a "single-
mother welfare" family, there is not much mystery
guessing what probably occurred. Nor what kind of
"justice" would be extracted.

Just plead guilty, it's worked out & you'll be O.K.
But if my son is not guilty?—what a travesty!
Quentin would not *do such a thing. He is my*
son, my boy & I know.

Quentin, O.K.? Agreed?

In fact Q__ P__ was visibly ashamed & repentant & had "learned his lesson"—one look at him, his grainy red-rimmed eyelids & parched lips, you knew.

Two years' sentence—suspended. Psychotherapy, counseling. Regular reporting to probation office. Agreed?

Tearful before Judge L__ & my hands in my pockets, in my right trouser pocket fingering my good-luck GOLD TOOTH & Dad whispered for me to take my hands out of my pockets, please. & I did, & I thanked Judge L__ for his understanding etc. as my lawyer advised. & leaving the judge's chambers I was having trouble breathing & Dad was gripping me by the elbow. *Buck up, son* those were his actual words *everything is fine now & we're going home.* & out in the empty courtroom, Mom & Grandma & Junie & Reverend Horn who is a close friend of Grandma's & who "vouched" for Q__ P__ to Judge L__ were waiting. I was wearing a new suit of small brown checks & a beige bowtie with narrow red stripes & my hair had been cut trimmed neat at the ears & the nape of the neck & I was not wearing my sexy aviator-style glasses but the clear plastic frames & I was not crying now but smiling & hugging my family the way you would do at such a time. I shook Reverend Horn's hand *Thank you, thank you I am so happy, so grateful. Thank you for your faith in me.*

We were outside then. A warm rain speckled my face.

It was then Dad handed me the car keys to his

1993 Lexus. Which I had never driven before. I understood it was to show how Dad trusts me, & the family trusts me & I would not let them down ever again. & driving out of the rundown city up along the lake to Dale Springs where the houses are spacious & set on large wooded lots & the streets are lined with trees & in good repair I felt such a sense of HOMECOMING & BEING LOVED & I kept just at the speed limit of 35 mph ignoring how other drivers tailgated & honked & passed me impatiently. Junie who is Big Sis to me even now aged thirty-five & principal of a junior high school, with a fond smile for her kid brother, said, *Quen was always the one of us who could drive a car* then adding quick, *—I mean is. Right, Quen?* I grinned into the rearview mirror. *Right, Junie.*

There has always been a special feeling between Big Sis & me. On her side at least.

Driving home, my old home I was welcome in at any time but had outgrown yes but Q__ P__ *is* welcome there at any time & maybe parental guidance is a good thing. One of those warm-rainy windy April days. The Great Lakes sky like folds of grayish-white brain matter. Dad beside me in the passenger's seat of this smooth terrific car & he's wearing a custom-made suit & looks good for an old guy his age stroking his chin where, a long time ago, his goatee had been. & in the back seat Mom, Grandma & Junie, chattering together & Mom's tears & the others comforting her & turning off onto Lakeview Boulevard bringing us home I almost could not remember why

I was so happy & feeling so free thinking of BLACK COCK, shy shrinking boy-penis like a baby rabbit, skinned. I'd held it tight in my hand tickling the tip with the tip of the ice pick but the pills hadn't taken effect yet for I was impatient & exhibited poor judgment (I see in retrospect—I was drunk) & the boy panicked beginning to bellow as he broke free like a frenzied animal crashing through the locked rear door of the Ford van SO HELP ME GOD I DON'T KNOW HOW. & running then naked but for his filthy T-shirt out into the street bellowing like a fire alarm rising louder & louder. MY ZOMBIE!

He had not asked for a nickel, he was trusting as a dog. Yet Q__ P__ could not trust *him*.

From the back seat they were asking me something & I wasn't listening the way you don't listen to females mostly but I must've answered O.K., maybe it was something about taking over as caretaker or maybe they liked my haircut. & Dad laid his hand on my shoulder. For the first time driving that day I believed I could feel the motion of the Earth. The Earth rushing through the emptiness of space. Spinning on its axis but they say you don't feel it, you can't experience it. But to feel it is to be scared & happy at once & to know that nothing matters but that you do what you want to do & what you do you *are*. & I knew I was moving into the future. There is no PAST anybody can get to, to alter things or even to know what those things were but there is definitely a future, we are already in it.

How Things Play Out

31

My name for him was SQUIRREL. That was my secret name & the name you may know of him is something else.

Q__ P__ did not mean for such to happen. SQUIRREL was not a wise choice of a specimen. I knew that, & have always known. I was resolute (how many times I have instructed myself!) SUCH WOULD NOT HAPPEN. Anyone with a family to care about him, Caucasian & suburban & living in Dale Springs!

Grandma is to blame for much of it. She would be hurt to know but that is so. Of course, not Q__ P__ her only grandson, nor anyone else, would ever disclose such a cruel truth to a woman so old.

Maybe I am wrong to say it is Grandma's *blame,* I think probably it is no one's. It is superstitious & retro to think in terms of *blame, fault, guilt.* Last night watching the TV coverage of Comet Shoemaker-Levy 9 hitting Jupiter confirmed this. Dad invited me over to the house to watch with them *this historic event* but I said Thanks Dad, I've got too much work to do (*work I am doing for* you, *Dad* was the message) & stayed in my shitty caretaker's quarters & ate my Hot Italian Sub from Enrico's & got pissed on a couple of bottles of dago red. They said the explosions on Jupiter were millions of times greater than any manmade explosion on Earth but it was just little black puffs going off on the screen. Flashes & fireballs & plumes of flame. Meteor trails how many millions or billions of miles away colliding with Jupiter's atmosphere & going off. Fragment Q hit about the time I nodded off.

How is there BLAME in those fireball plumes. If they explode on Jupiter or Earth. If they are fated by the Universe since the beginning of time or manmade. So there is no BLAME in Grandma. I am wrong to be pissed at a woman so old. Who is so good to me.

It was like this. Grandma requested would I drive her to places because she does not drive a car any longer & that was O.K. by me—sometimes. (For Grandma paid me, of course.) Would I drive her to some other old woman's house, or to visit some pathetic old cripples in some nursing home & wait around for her & drive her back home & that was O.K. If I was free & didn't have too much caretaker shit to do at the house or homework from Dale Tech. (In fact the semester was over, the courses were ended.) & then Grandma got the idea to hire me for yard work, mow the lawn (which is approximately one half-acre) & trim the hedge & sprinkle fertilizer in the rose beds etc. & that was O.K. in theory. Grandma would pay me $50 to $75 cash for just a few hours' work & I did not need to be too thorough, she never came out to examine it. An operation for cataracts or something in one or both of her eyes so maybe she couldn't see too well & I didn't inquire. Grandma slipped these bills to me saying *This is just between you & me, Quentin. Our little secret!* meaning not Dad nor the IRS would know.

Maybe Grandma was lonely & that was why. Trying to get me to stay for supper etc. There was another old woman, a widow who was a friend of Grandma's & sometimes I would drive this other old woman to *her* home & she would tip me, too. Like a taxi service. In my 1987 Ford van with the American flag decal in the rear window.

32

Even before SQUIRREL it was a season of many plans!—buzzing my head like ideas from outer space! I would wake in my van not knowing where I was in a parking lot of some tavern in some city unrecognizable to me & it's morning & fierce pounding sunshine in my eyes like spikes—& in a cold calm check the rear of the van, the neatly folded plastic garbage bags & plastic sheets etc., & discover no evidence. Or I would wake in my caretaker's quarters but not in bed, on the sofa fully clothed except unzipped & my hard cock poking free, the TV going loud & it's morning of some day unknown to me, empty bottles or beer cans underfoot, & roaches scurrying over the pizza crusts & bells of such sweetness chiming from the Music College, it was like something MIRACULOUS had happened in my sleep! A voice said *If you go down into the cellar, Quentin, he awaits you.*

Who? Who awaits me?

You know who.

My ZOMBIE? My ZOMBIE?

But the voice disappeared into the TV ads & footsteps overhead & plumbing. & next-door in the kitchen Big Black Guy (as I called him) from Zaire thumping at roaches with a rolled-up newspaper. As I have requested him not to do.

Knowing then it is just Q__ P__ alone in the Universe. If you want something to happen, *you* do it.

33

There was talk of Q__ enrolling for summer session at the tech college but the registration days came & went. I had informed Dad & Mom & Mr. T__ that I had passed both courses & liked the college O.K. but wasn't decided yet about continuing. & Dad got excited saying *What of your future, son?—you are over thirty years old, you can't be a caretaker all your life can you* & the word "caretaker" on his tongue like a turd. & I said. & Dad said. & Mom said the fall was a long way off & no decision had to be made quickly. So that was how the discussion ended that day.

An envelope from Dale College came to Q__ P__ at 118 North Church Street, a transcript of my grades probably. I ripped it up without opening it & tossed the pieces away.

34

Mowing Grandma's lawn one Saturday in July &
trimming the evergreen hedge & I heard kids shout-
ing & laughing next door in the neighbors' swimming pool. DON'T LOOK the voice said calmly. But
it was a tease. It seemed to know beforehand. Five
or six teenaged kids including one boy about fifteen just blew my mind, his swim trunks streaming
water when he climbed out of the pool after diving
a perfect dive & his young muscle-hard body like
something shining I couldn't take my eyes off. & I
made my way along the hedge to get a better look
& it went through me like a knife seeing his face.
Enough like Barry's face to be his TWIN! Except
Barry was younger in my memory of course & dark-
haired, & this boy was older, tall & lean & quick &
loud & his hair a fairer brown like streaked from
the sun.

Barry, my friend from seventh grade at Dale
Springs Junior High which was just a mile or so from
Grandma's house!—the buff-brick building I'd drive
by on my way to Grandma's, only a block or so out
of my way.

Barry who'd drowned in a swimming accident at the school, struck his head on the side of the pool & sank & so many kids yelling & wild tossing volleyballs it wasn't noticed till we were almost all out of the pool. How many months, years later I overheard Mom say to one of her women friends on the telephone *Quentin is still mourning that poor child's death, I don't think he will ever get over it.*

Newspaper clippings I saved for years, photos of Barry alone & with his basketball teammates in the special memorial issue of the school newspaper, & a grimy sock of Barry's I had taken from his locker, kept in one of my SECRET PLACES between my mattress & bed springs & one night reaching for the sock to fondle I discovered my treasure was gone. & whoever had taken it, Mom, or Dad, never spoke to me of it. Nor did I give any sign.

& NOW BARRY WAS RETURNED TO ME! But golden-shining in the sun & in fact better-looking, sexy that way young teenaged boys are so self-assured & swaggering with their buddies & showing off to girls. "SQUIRREL" was my immediate name for him, that blond-brown-streaked hair & his energy & clowning-around & loud giggle. "SQUIRREL" just came to me & so it was. This could not be just chance. Q__ P__ struck like somebody'd hit me over the head with a hammer. & my cock alert, in wonderment.

For here was my true ZOMBIE. No questions asked.

Q__ P__ calm & collected though returning to the hedge etc. Taking up the clippers & continuing work. All thoughts of dark-haired dark-skinned specimens, Ramid & Akhil & Abdellah & the rest beneath the roof at 118 North Church & even Velvet Tongue flushed away in those quick seconds like shit down a toilet.

35

This property Q__ P__ is CARETAKER for why can't I be such for life, if I so wish?

The P__ family house, large & dignified red-brick Victorian, 118 North Church Street, Mt. Vernon, Michigan. None of the P__ family live here now except Q__ P__ CARETAKER.

It is a job that suits me. Like Mr. T__ says, such responsibility is good for a man.

It was after World War II Grandma says University Heights began to change. *Coloreds* began to move in & *whites* to move out in a steady irreversible stream to such suburbs as Dale Springs. *Oh I will never forgive the Germans for that war!* Grandma says.

The foundation of our house was laid 1892 & it is still firm. The cellar Grandpa P__ had renovated in the 1950s (as I have been told, I was not born yet) is such that there are two sections: the new, & the old. The new has a poured concrete floor & reinforced walls with beaverboard paneling. The gas furnace is here, water heater, fuse box, washer-drier etc. CARETAKER's work bench & such tools as my electric power drill & newly purchased Cherokee chainsaw.

The old section of the cellar is never used. Not as large as the new but it is still sizable, approximately the length & width of the kitchen. A hard-packed dirt floor & the ceiling rafters low (not six feet from the floor) & filthy with cobwebs. Walls termite-ridden & rotted. Except for seepage the cistern is dry of course, not used for forty years. A strong smell of drains in the rainy months but I have installed a second pump. Convinced Dad it was necessary to maintain the property, & it is.

To penetrate the depths of the old cellar you must move slowly & cautiously, stooped over. You need a strong flashlight. You need sharp eyes. You need to be able to go without breathing deeply because of the smell. You need a will not easily broken.

It has been months now & the cistern has almost been converted & will be ready for use soon. Though I will have some awkwardness I guess getting my "operating table" into it—a folding table, a dinette from the Salvation Army where I got my locker is probably the best bet.

My locker I should mention is in my room. Scrubbed clean & sprayed with Lysol & used for clothes, shoes, etc., & the quart bottle of formaldehyde containing a good-luck memento from BIG GUY & the bottle itself carefully wrapped in aluminum foil & taped. & magazines, videos, Polaroids, etc. Always kept locked.

The old cellar & the cistern are the crucial places of course. A healthy ZOMBIE might live for many years there for who would know of him? who except Q__ P__, CARETAKER? & if a ZOMBIE is a failure there is the earthen floor for safe & sanitary disposal. & there is a new door replacing the old rotted door & last week I purchased a steel padlock from Sears for added security.

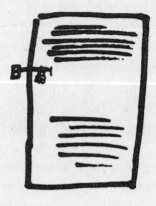

36

Q_ P_ CRAZY FOR SQUIRREL !!!

—I wrote in red Magic Marker inside a toilet stall in the Humpty Dumpty on Lakeview Boulevard, Dale Springs, where SQUIRREL worked as a busboy. It blew my mind to think SQUIRREL would use the toilet & puzzle over those very words with no clue who "SQUIRREL" was let alone "Q__ P__"!

How many strangers' eyes would fix upon "Q__ P__ CRAZY FOR SQUIRREL!!!" with no comprehension what these words mean. What a fantastic fireball-power in my cock.

SQUIRREL's busboy schedule at Humpty Dumpty (near as I could determine) was Wed.–Thurs.–Fri. 12 noon to 6 P.M. Summer work I guess. One evening parked in my van in the parking lot & waiting for SQUIRREL I saw him exit at the rear at 6:06 P.M. & there was a woman (probably his mother) in a station wagon picking him up but other times he rode his bicycle (kept at the rear with two or three other employees' bicycles all chain-locked) to his home on Cedar Street, a distance of 2.3 miles. SQUIRREL did not live next door to Grandma as I had originally surmised but was often at that house, swimming in his friend's pool & listening to loud rock music & goofing off like adolescent kids will do. (A good sign, SQUIRREL was *not* a next-door neighbor of Grandma's. For next-door neighbors are always among the first to be questioned by the police.) It was easy to trail SQUIRREL home on his bicycle.

It is easy to trail anyone home, of your choosing. No need even to be INVISIBLE.

I learned the family name. & telephoned once or twice just to hear the phone ring in that house. A female voice answered (his "Mom"?) & I asked for him (his name which does not suit him, much) & left only the message *This is Q___. I will call back.* There are two younger children in the family, at least. & "Mom" & "Dad" of some age around forty. "Mom" like any other woman on such a street as Cedar Street, Dale Springs & "Dad" the executive-type drives a Buick Riviera & carries a briefcase. So far as I could figure, SQUIRREL is a student at Dale Springs High, Q___ P___'s old school he hated & wished to have burnt to the ground. With everybody in it.

The address is 166 Cedar, Grandma's address is 149 Arden. Parallel streets & the same kinds of houses, mostly colonials in wooded lots like Grandma's. SQUIRREL's family's house is pretty big, with a white picket fence & giant trees—elms? oaks?—& Grandma's house is smaller, with a part-fieldstone facade. Grandma came to live here when Grandpa died about ten years ago. To be near her son & daughter-in-law. & the other day at Grandma's where

she made me blueberry waffles (a late breakfast before I started the yard work) it came to me that
Grandma was an old woman & would not live much
longer. & she would be leaving an estate of course.
This house, & her savings & investments & there was
the rental property at 118 North Church worth how
much?—$80,000? $100,000? In all, Grandma would
leave a sizable estate. Maybe she would leave something to her grandson & granddaughter? In recent
months I was led to believe that I was her favorite &
not Junie any longer. But I could be mistaken—with
females & their feelings about one another you can't
tell.

In any case Grandma P__ would leave a sizable estate when she died to Mr. & Mrs. R__ P__. & they
would not live forever, either.

It seemed right that Q__ P__ CARETAKER should
inherit the house on North Church. Maybe the old
woman has had such a thought herself by now. *This
is just between you & me Quentin. Our little secret!*

Standing on tiptoe to pat my cheek. A fattish
old woman but frail, too. They say their bones are
weak, hollowed out inside & easy to break. Her
washed-out no-color eyes I had a weird flash minia-
ture QUENTINS were mirrored in! For once they
have loved you as their baby, their own strange flesh
born of their bodies or their children's bodies,
always you are BABY in their eyes.

37

A plan was forming like a slow dream & I did not push or hurry it. Though knowing SQUIRREL's summer schedule would end by Labor Day. Which left how many weeks for Q__ P__ to make his capture?—only about five. & SQUIRREL worked at Humpty Dumpty only three days a week.

Now in the heat of Michigan summer I quit my medication totally & had less timidity of EYE CONTACT I saw things normally not-seen. & they sank deep in me, & brooded. *A responsible man makes his own luck* Dad has said. Quoting one of the great philosophers.

From that Saturday at Grandma's spying on my prey through the hedge I knew I would have my SQUIRREL. I never doubted. He could tease & taunt me diving in the pool, & yelling & laughing running & streaming water in his tight swim trunks & at the Humpty Dumpty he could look through me like nobody was seated in the booth in which I sat but that would not forestall what would happen. Fragment Q of the big comet pulled apart into clusters of fire by drifting too near Jupiter & that terrible gravitational field & it would collide with its target & explode & it was fated to be so & it would be so. From the beginning of Time.

Except: Q__ P__'s strategy would be 100% different than in the past. This was Dale Springs & not the inner city, nor any lonely stretch of interstate. This was a Caucasian upper-middle-class kid, a child (as his parents probably considered him) & not a black or a mixed breed & lots of people cared for, & would miss at once. & would notify the police in a panic. For sure.

& that excited me, too. For never in the past not once to my knowledge had any cops anywhere known of my specimens' disappearance, let alone searched for them. & so this would be different, & I believed I would be equal to the challenge. So wild a need & hunger, SQUIRREL entering my life like a shining angel—he was worth dying for, for sure!

Because SQUIRREL would not likely be hitch-hiking in Dale Springs & it would not be likely Q__ P__ would drive by in his van, one chance in one million BUT I COULD NOT WAIT THAT LONG COULD I!—another strategy had to be devised. SQUIRREL would not climb willingly into the van, SQUIRREL would have to be overcome & captured & lifted into it, & his bicycle too?—maybe. & this capture to be made without witnesses of course. By night would be best but to stake out at his house on Cedar Street not knowing when he would return & not knowing if he would be alone would be difficult. For the sand-colored van would be noticed. Dale Springs has security police, neighborhood patrols. & to enter SQUIRREL's actual house & risk a burglar alarm etc.—fuck *that*.

I worked at Grandma's & I cruised my van on Cedar Street & I ate at Humpty Dumpty how many times, not able to stay away, & I brooded over SQUIRREL in his absence & in his presence. Staring at SQUIRREL thinking *I love you, I want you, I would die for you, you are so terrific why the fuck won't you look at me? smile at me?* I might have neglected my duties at 118 North Church but it was summer & only five of the rooms occupied & if I did not haul the trash out to the curb one week I would haul it the next, for sure. & cleaning & maintenance got done when required. & regular spray for roach control.

Dad called & left a message & I thought he'd be bitching as usual but instead thanked me for BEING SO KIND TO YOUR GRANDMA, QUEN-TIN!

It was taking a chance eating at Humpty Dumpty so much but I could not stay away. Parked my van sometimes in the lot & sometimes across the street or close by in a grocery store lot or even around the corner to avoid suspicion. But the restaurant lot was always full & the restaurant busy except in the mid-afternoon but I preferred after 5 P.M. when there were lots of customers including families with young children & less likelihood of Q__ P__ being noticed. & if I lingered till 6 P.M. when the busboys changed shifts I could observe SQUIRREL actually leaving, riding home on his bicycle. That route he took, I'd memorized.

Following in my van at a safe distance. Or, circling the block to park & wait for him to pass oblivious. The way SQUIRREL rode his bicycle!—fast, & hunched over, & no wasted moves. Very shrewd & skillful making his way through Lakeview Boulevard traffic. & a shortcut he took through a side street & an alley & the rear of a church parking lot. A Tigers baseball cap backward on his head & his blond-brown longish hair tied in a tiny pigtail at the nape of his neck & how boylike he was but a man too, almost a man, his mouth that could shape into a grin or a sneer, his eyes that could be so warm or so cutting & the way he gripped the handlebars of the bicycle & his muscled calves, thighs & the curve of his spine back how elastic his spine looked—it took my breath away this boy would be my ZOMBIE!

Then in Humpty Dumpty watching SQUIRREL hoist a tray of dirty dishes, etc. to his shoulder. & his young muscles jerking visible, & the little pigtail at the nape of his neck—

& I'm so excited have to leave my Humpty Dumpty Burger Special & stagger back to the men's room & jack off in one of the toilet stalls moaning & whimpering. *A true ZOMBIE would be mine forever. Would kneel before me saying I LOVE YOU MASTER, THERE IS NO ONE BUT YOU MASTER. FUCK ME IN THE ASS MASTER UNTIL I BLEED BLUE GUTS.* & I wipe the sticky cum in wads of tissue & return to the booth where I will leave it hidden inside my napkin for SQUIRREL to clear away unknowing.

MY ZOMBIE!

I was not too hungry (having eaten at Grandma's) yet devoured two Tex-Mex Specials, burgers with melted cheese, onions & hot salsa sauce & double order of Humpty Dumpty Special Ranch Fries greasy & coated with salt. Two giant Cokes & cups of black coffee for a caffeine buzz. & the uppers I'd taken that morning. Dazed & shaky from jerking off so hard & my vision fading in & out of focus & the gum-chewing waitress asked me something—*Mister?* I didn't seem to hear & shrugged & sauntered away. But where was SQUIRREL? I did not see SQUIRREL! A roaring in my ears & rock music piped in overhead & kids' voices & laughter echoing like inside my own skull. Then SQUIRREL appeared & was helping another busboy clean up a booth where it looked like pigs had been feeding, wiping with sponges & tossing napkins, Styrofoam cups etc. into a plastic basket. The other busboy was SQUIRREL's age & the two of them buddies, grinning together. (If they should look over at Q__ P__ watching them, how would they react?) SQUIRREL is smart & sexy & knows it for sure. A better muscle-build than his friend, too. His skin is slightly blemished on his jaws & he has a habit of grimacing & rolling his eyes, that mocking look you see in kids that age. Some friends of his come into the restaurant & there's wisecrack bantering & insults traded. *Why didn't Q__ P__ have friends like that, guys who liked me, guys like brothers? twins?* & now when they see me their eyes flick carelessly over me. Little cocksuckers don't see *me* at all.

My hand was shaky!—dropped my fork & it clattered to the floor as SQUIRREL was passing near. Quick & polite SQUIRREL got me a clean fork, I didn't even have to ask. *Here y'are mister!* with a smile. & I said *O.K. thanks!* & though I lifted my eyes to his there was no eye contact, SQUIRREL was already moving on. A clear glimpse of his greenish-cool eyes, though. Like no other eyes I have ever seen. MY ZOMBIE.

Hadn't noticed me at all, I guess. & that was good. They don't see people my age, that's good. Sure I was hurt, I was pissed & *the little fucker will pay for it one day soon* but it *was* good. Q__ P__ the invisible man.

What I was wearing: khaki shorts & a soiled tank-top (loose-fitting to hide my little pot-belly), & my aviator sunglasses, & battered sandals. Working at Grandma's I'd worn a red sweatband around my head like a funky black dude, I'd sweated it through in the heat. A strong smell lifted off me I guess, hadn't taken time to shower as Grandma had invited.

My *baffle* that day was a birthmark on my left cheek. Inscribed with blueberry juice & red Magic Marker. Sort of star-shaped, about the size of a dime. To draw & focus unwanted attention.

 BIRTHMARK (ACTUAL SIZE)

The waitress brought me my check, it came to $16.95 & I left a $5 tip. "Make sure the busboy gets some of this," I told the waitress.

"Excuse me?"

"The busboy. That kid there, with the pigtail. I'm leaving a $5 tip & I want him to get his share."

The waitress slowed her gum-chewing & stared at me & blinked & colored a little like, for sure, she'd been caught stealing. Cunt had been planning to pocket the $5 herself. Saying, "We all share our tips here, mister. That's policy."

"O.K. I'm just inquiring."

"That's Humpty Dumpty policy, mister. We all share."

"O.K.," I said, sliding out of the booth, on my unsteady legs & the sunglasses sliding down my nose, "—that's cool. That's just fine."

If SQUIRREL was looking on, & gazed after Q__ P__ walking away with his head high, I could only guess.

38

Q__ P__ a PERPETUAL HARD-ON.

So much strangeness raining on my head that summer!—like the 21 "bright pearls" of the Comet EXPLODING one by one in my head! & the promise of more, & MORE!

& I was seeing with NEW EYES, & needed but a few hours' sleep crowded with plans, & such muscle-energy & zest & hope for the capture of the prey & MY ZOMBIE awaiting in Grandpa's old cistern!

Even Dr. E__ who usually yawned through our fifty minutes & removed his glasses to rub his piss-colored eyes took note. Speaking of a *healthy tone* to my skin & inquired how things were going in my life? & I said things were going real well doctor, smiling shyly but like I meant it, no bullshit & I'm proud & Dr. E__ then inquired was I taking my medication faithfully, with meals three times a day? & said yes doctor & next he asks if I was dreaming yet? did I recall any dreams? & I said yes doctor so he looked at me blinking like I was a dog suddenly up on my hind legs & speaking English.

"*You*, Quentin? *You* had a dream?"

"Yes, doctor."

"What was it about?"

"Baby chicks."

"Excuse me?"

"Baby chicks. Little chickens."

There was a pause, & Dr. E__ pushed his glasses against the bridge of his nose & continued to look at me. Those piss-eyes alert & wondering, the first time in sixteen months. "Well—what did you dream about the baby chicks, Quentin?"

"I don't know," I said, & this was true, at that time, "—they were just there."

Feeling so good afterward I almost—almost!—told Dr. E__ I had no further need of him & his shit-prescription he could stuff up his ass.

& later that day which was Tuesday, & SQUIR-REL would not be working at Humpty Dumpty & it was a muggy-drizzly day so he would not be at his friend's swimming pool next-door to Grandma's, I was walking fast across the University campus making a detour as always around Erasmus Hall & I was wearing my khaki shorts & a loose-fitting MT. VERNON U. T-shirt & my aviator glasses & caught some quizzical eyes I believe & some registering of approval. Summer school was in session & the kids in clothes like mine. Except of course the old-fart profs you always encounter on campus & they're staring at you like you are a freak or a Nazi. Or worse. But I was feeling high after last night's BABY CHICK dream & puzzling what it might

mean & sure the answer would come to me, &
soon.

& in Darwin Hall where I hadn't been for years &
years climbing to the third floor like I knew where I
was going. Poked my head into a big lecture hall &
that wasn't it. Poked my head into Dept. of Biology
Office & that wasn't it. Poked my head into a lab
smelling strong enough to make my eyes sting &
that *was* it. Where years ago I'd seen stacked cages
of cats, rabbits, monkeys with electrodes in their
skulls. Some of them unmoving in their cages &
some turning & twisting. Some of them sightless
though their eyes glittered. & all of them soundless
though opening their mouths & emitting silent
cries set the air to vibrating though unheard. It
must've been Dad who'd brought me?—or I'd wan-
dered away from Dad in another place & pushed
into the lab AUTHORIZED PERSONNEL ONLY: DEPT. OF
BIOLOGY drawn by the smell. Yet that day it was just
a lab, a long room with sinks & counters & instruments etc. & the wall of cages was gone. & a young
Asian-looking female grad student who's alone in
the room blinks at me like she's a little scared of me
which is O.K. by Q__ P__, that's the only kind of
female you can trust. So I ask where are the animals
& she says what animals & I say there used to be
cats, rabbits, monkeys in this lab & you were exper-
imenting on them & she says when was this? & I say
a few years ago & she says she's only been here two
years & doesn't know anything about it & things
are changed now in the department. & she was sort
of backing up & I saw she would back up against a

117

big-screen computer on a table & she did & could not back up any farther so I thought DON'T: DON'T ALARM THE CUNT & I did not press forward farther but changed tone as I can do, I am skilled at doing & getting better every day. Is she a biology student I ask & she says she's a biogeneticist doing research for her Ph.D. & I say I am a physics grad student doing research for my Ph.D., I am Professor R__ P__'s assistant. & she looks at me with her flat face & dark-slanted eyes & I see she doesn't know who the fuck R__ P__ is! Which is a laugh. A real laugh. & Erasmus Hall just across the quad. So I'm a little short of breath & run my hands through my hair which is greasy & like quills but I don't press any farther forward. & we go:

"Where are vocal cords exactly?"

"Excuse me?"

"Vocal cords. Where are vocal cords exactly?"

"Vocal cords? Like in—your throat?"

"Human vocal cords, but I'm talking about animals," I say. I am speaking calmly, reasonably. You would know I was a fellow scientist by my demeanor. "Lab animals' vocal cords are cut, aren't they? How is it done?"

& she's looking at me a little scared again & uncertain. Saying, "I don't do that kind of research."

& I say, "I don't either, I'm a Ph.D. in physics I said. But how is it done? Is it easy, or tricky?"

& Flatface shakes her head like she doesn't know. & I'm getting a little pissed but not showing it. Saying, "O.K., where are your vocal cords exactly?"

& Flatface puts her fingers to her throat like she's checking does she have any. "You can feel them," she says. "They vibrate when you touch them, when you speak."

39

QUANTIFIABLE & UNQUANTIFIABLE MATERIAL!

For a long time, how many fucking years of Q__ P__'s life it had seemed maybe, like a scientific experiment, like it was a principle of shifting to the left or the right for instance, a few inches & no more. Or growing taller. & all the Universe would re-arrange. & others were born with radar for such but not Q__ P__. The principle (though not articulated at the time, being too young) of pushing up close be-hind the boys in the cafeteria line, Bruce & his friends. Or entering the showers in high school at the right instant, with just the right stride & angle of head & shoulders. & yesterday purchasing three dozen baby chicks at this farmers' market in Luding-ton *for that was something Q__ P__ had never be-fore done in his life & to do it just once was to be somebody new.* Or, those months at Eastern Michi-gan U. where Q__ P__ strove to RE-INVENT MYSELF purchasing clothes & shoes not of his own taste but that of others closely observed, & showering twice a day (for a while, until my skin began to flake away like scales) & even forcing a new handwriting & new signature which it required many weeks to master. But it *was* mastered!

Quentin

Some shift to the left, or right, or up, or down, or in thickness, or in thinness. Some alteration of skin tone, or freckles. Or a more baritone voice not reedy & nasal any longer. & Q__ P__ would be pledged to DEKE for instance! But what seemed so easy was in fact so hard.

If you had a heart, that is how it would be broken.

& the other day driving Mom & Grandma to this nursing home in Holland, Mich. Presbyterian auspices. Where they visited some old shriveled female relative & brought her potted dyed-blue flowers & I paced around the lobby for a while then outside in the parking lot & somebody in a wheelchair & their family glancing at me & finally one of them says, a youngish guy but his voice quavering, *Excuse me? Would you please not stare at my mother?* & on campus that day so charged up seeing SQUIRREL-SQUIRREL-SQUIRREL in every kid of a certain height & figure my cock was hard as a club & hair erect as quills & I had to seek a men's room to jerk off before EXPLODING. & I'm pushing through some doors & there's a lighted stage & some guys & females in leggings or whatever are rehearsing some dance to kettle drums & horns & they're so absorbed in their

121

dancing they don't see Q__ P__'s eyes glaring up at them out of the shadow. & finally somebody comes over to me, some faculty cunt, female with thick glasses & asks who am I please? & I turn to her not-surprised & say, like this is the most natural reply to an asshole question, *I am the presence standing here at this juncture of Time & Space—who else?*

& that night in my sand-colored 1987 Ford van with the American flag decal covering the rear window cruising Cedar Street, Dale Springs & parked in shadow & with my binoculars trained to the mostly shaded or darkened windows I thought, *If this is where I am this is* who *I am.* & so it was.

40

HOW THINGS PLAY OUT. July 28 telephoned Dad's lawyer he'd hired for me last year, hadn't been in contact since that day we walked out of Judge L__'s chambers. Saying in a fast voice *Don't tell my Dad please! I'm kind of scared the cops are tailing me, harassing me, not in actual actions nor in words but day & night there's squad cars cruising North Church Street. & I have reason to believe they have questioned some of the tenants of this house. & if the tenants move out* my voice was rising, panting, *& Dad takes away my caretaker job—WHAT WILL I DO?*

Purchased a second-hand folding "dinette" table. Not at the Salvation Army downtown but a furniture outlet in Grand Rapids. The man helped me carry it & load into the rear of the van. *Hey don't you want the chairs?—four chairs come with it.* & I say, *Chairs? Why?*

Purchased rubber gloves of the ordinary household kind. The kind for dishwashing. Purchased a roll of gauze in a drugstore. To prepare a surgical mask.

Fed & watered baby chicks. In three cardboard cartons with airholes. I'd run a long extension cord into the old cellar & it's handy. The farmer advised keeping them warm with 50-watt bulbs one to each box. CHEEP CHEEP CHEEPING. Tiny beaks & clawed feet, & yellow fuzz-feathers looking like they're dyed. You don't think of Easter chicks born this time of year.

41

Final week in July. My will power is such I stay away from Humpty Dumpty Wed. & Thurs. but there I am, Fri. & SQUIRREL is not on the premises that I can see. & I almost freak. In my booth at the farthest rear corner near the swinging kitchen doors. & I'm wearing a Tigers baseball cap backward on my head & dark plastic shades over my regular glasses & my blueberry-stain birthmark & NO SQUIRREL. Has he quit, is he gone? How will I hook up with him again? Oh Christ. Oh God if You exist help me now!

& the kitchen doors swing open with a blast of heat & smelly air—& THERE SQUIRREL IS!

Time 5:07 P.M., date July 29.

My jumpy eyes lowered to my plate where I'm eating Humpty Dumpty Special Fried Chicken Parts & Special Ranch Fries & Homemade Coleslaw but I track SQUIRREL in the corner of my eye where he's clearing tables of dirty dishes etc. Perspiration gleaming on his upper lip. *If you would look at me. If you would smile. Just once!* But like Barry he does not see *me*. Like Bruce, he does not see *me*. & there's three young girls in shorts & halter tops &

125

sliding curtains of shiny hair in one of the booths. & they're teasing SQUIRREL who's their friend. & he's blushing self-conscious in his soiled apron. Yes but loving it—for sure. MY ZOMBIE strutting like a proud little cock before such cunts! & a sidelong smile at them showing his dazzle-teeth & a dimple in his right cheek I had not seen before & I swallow a mouthful of gristle & almost choke & the little cunts shiver & giggle together like the three of them are coming at the same time squirming their asses on the vinyl seat. & SQUIRREL strutting past with a big tray of dishes on his shoulder, their master.

MY ZOMBIE betraying me in full view!

At 5:58 P.M. Q__ P__ left Humpty Dumpty & crossed to the van parked inconspicuously at the rear of the Lakeview Food Mart. A busy place this Friday evening. & in the van idling the motor for a minute then easing out into eastbound traffic & there shortly emerges SQUIRREL pedaling his bicycle east along Lakeview. & keeping in the right-hand lane I follow at a safe distance slow like I'm looking for a parking space. Note how SQUIRREL turns as usual south on a narrow side street Locust & I don't follow where he turns into a one-way alley (parallel with Lakeview, a half-block in) & proceeds eastward toward the rear of St. Agnes Roman Catholic Church past the point of GROUND ZERO (where the van will be parked for the capture). Instead I accelerate & at Pearl turn right, which is south, & pass the church & the adjoining cemetery & there in my rearview mirror after a minute or so appears SQUIRREL again pedaling oblivious! Like he is in a movie, & does not know it. But I know it. & I park at the curb & allow him to pass me. His strong legs pedaling, & his lean back bent over like in a swoon! & I follow him slowly & cross Arden (where Grandma lives a block away, east) & two streets down to Cedar (where SQUIRREL lives a block & a half away, east) & SQUIRREL turns onto Cedar & I continue south on Pearl. *Just between you & me. Our little secret.*

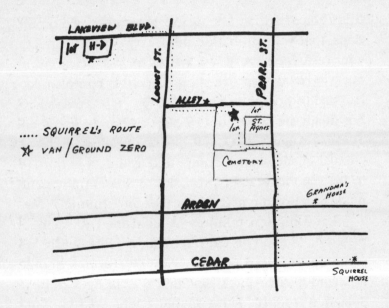

42

It is a requirement, Michigan Department of Corrections, that your probation officer comes to "inspect" your residence every few weeks, or maybe months. Mr. T__ who was overworked (as he complained) had had to postpone his visit to Q__ P__'s residence but finally he came to 118 North Church Street on Tuesday August 2. Q__ P__ who pleaded guilty of "sexual misdemeanor committed against a minor" is in his second year of probation & his employment record, deportment & medical record "model." Mr. T__ had only ten minutes he explained & seemed pissed, talking on his car phone for a while before he came up the steps & *Well hello, Quentin!* & shook my hand in that quick pinching way of his like he's detached from his hand & your contamination. Lifting his eyes inside his bifocals & he's impressed with the P__ family house you can tell. University Heights neighborhood. *He'd* gone to Western Michigan State in Kalamazoo.

I opened the door & Mr. T__ preceded me inside & he was saying in a loud voice like talking to a mental defective *So you're responsible for all this, eh? Good for you Quen-tin.* Showed him the front parlor where there's a sofa & chairs & a TV for use of the tenants. Showed him the kitchen where tenants have "kitchen privileges." I had cleaned up the dirty dishes & even scoured the sink & there was a strong stink of insecticide but no roaches in evidence. Not opening the cupboard doors where things were shoved inside. Opened the refrigerator like for something to do & Mr. T__ might've sighed exhaling his breath through his teeth. *Just great, Quen-tin. So* where do *you* live? Showed him my room at the rear. Q__ P__ CARETAKER in black ink on a white card beside the door. The window air conditioner was rattling & the vent open & I believe the room did not smell too strongly of whatever it might smell of. (My own nostrils were accustomed to whatever this might be, thus not reliable.) Sweat-stiffened socks & underwear needing to be laundered, & damp towels etc. The gray scum of the bathroom sink & toilet & shower stall. But the bed was neatly made & the cover (a purchase of Mom's) of navy blue with tiny ships & anchors & flying fish drawn to the pillow which was in a straight position. The single window needing to be washed outside & in overlooking the weedy back yard I had not mowed in weeks, working at Grandma's so much. But Mr. T__ took little notice. Nor of the twelve stones atop the air conditioner. I opened my closet door voluntarily & there on hooks were—for a weird moment I saw my fucked-up ZOMBIES!—my clothes, which were not many but some fancy & funky—RAISINEYES' leather slouch-brim hat on the shelf, & a zebra-stripe shirt of BIG GUY's (too big for Q__ P__), & some leather neckties, lizardskin belts, the sheepskin jacket & on the floor my prize kidskin boots courtesy of Rooster. I opened my locker door too & there was my calendar taped to the inside of the door with certain markings ★ ★ ★ & my T-shirts, work-shorts, jogging shoes etc. A strong clean smell of Lysol. In an aluminum foil bag like you bring home a roasted chicken to heat in the oven in, the quart bottle of form- aldehyde containing my prize memento of BIG GUY but the object was neatly taped of course & gave off no odor or suspicion. I have not opened it to glance at it for a long time. Mr. T__ did not so much as glance at any of this either for why should he. Q__ P__ has nothing to hide, the five or six knives & the ice pick etc. & the pistol locked in the cellar. Mr. T__ saying *Great, Quen-tin. Very neat & clean. Just right for you, eh?* Saying, *A little responsibility makes a man feel good, eh?* My muscle-mags & porn stuff I'd hidden away. & my Polaroids. & the map of SQUIRREL's bicycle route. Instead, there was a neat stack of many issues of the *Dale Tech Blaze* & brown grocery bags carefully smoothed & folded on the floor. *Just like my wife,* Mr. T__ said. *Those damned grocery bags!* On my bedside table *Elements of Geophysics* & Mr. T__ picked it up & glanced inside seeing the name. *Second-hand, eh? All my books were second-hand, too. Couldn't afford new.* Asked me about my classes at Dale Tech & I told him what I had told him before & he said it was a good school, his sister's son got a degree in electrical engineering & has a good entry-level job with GE in Lansing.

In the front hall I was walking Mr. T___ to the door there was Abdellah & Akhil at the mailboxes & they were chattering together & their eyes & teeth flashing & went quiet at once as Mr. T___ (who is a big slope-bellied white man with a flushed face & balding scalp) bore upon them & murmured *Excuse me!* & eased past in the narrow space. & Abdellah & Akhil went upstairs quiet now. & Mr. T___ said nothing until we were out onto the porch then said, *Must be a little weird for a white man, white caretaker, for* them, *eh?* & adding quickly *I don't mean anything by it, I've got lots of black friends. I'm speaking of history.*

43

On the air conditioner in Q__ P__'s CARETAKER quarters were nine small stones from the back yard. There had been fifteen originally.

As the days passed. & GROUND ZERO located somewhere within those remaining days of August.

August 9. Dad & Mom called & left a joint message. They would be away for two weeks as usual on Mackinac Island. *Sorry you don't care to join us Quentin! But if you should change your mind—* & I pressed the button ERASE.

August 11. Junie called. I was in the old cellar preparing the "operating" room in the cistern & came upstairs for a beer & there was Junie's scolding voice just recording. Saying she'd been expecting me to return her calls & *why haven't you Quentin. Are you O.K. Quentin. Is anything wrong Quentin. You are not drinking again Quentin are you. Please call back.*

ERASE.

HOW THINGS PLAY OUT. A certain juncture of TIME & SPACE. A certain minute of a day of a life & a stretch of a one-way alley of security fences, high hedges & rears of buildings. (The site I chose for the van & the capture was behind a commercial building FOR SALE & the rear entrance & garage never used. No private residences nearby. Always the chance of somebody driving through the alley, other kids on bikes etc. but that was a chance Q__ P__ must take.) & NO TURNING BACK.

44

Six stones remaining on the air conditioner. & then five, & then four. FRAGMENT Q primed to EXPLODE but: when?

Thursday August 25 would be the date, I thought. GROUND ZERO & on my calendar taped inside my locker door I marked it in red Magic Marker: ★

How many times Q__ P__ awaits SQUIRREL his prey in his van calm & methodical. & how many times Q__ P__ *is* SQUIRREL pedaling his bicycle fast & jaunty & graceful & oblivious to all danger like a deer running & leaping & the hunter's scope trained to his heart. SQUIRREL with his TIGERS cap backward on his blond-brown hair & his lean shoulders hunched over the lowered handlebars & the belt & waist of his jeans so narrow it looked like I could circle my fingers around him. & that little pigtail! & his tanned good-looking face lifted, the forehead slightly creased in that way you see in kids & it surprises you, a kid thinking let alone worrying. Like SQUIRREL knows himself the bearer of a SPECIAL

DESTINY. & I saw the knobby vertebrae of his spine & a shiver ran through me.

No! he is too beautiful for Q__ P__ to touch!

Jerking off every few hours, too wired to sit still & too excited to go out & risk somebody seeing me & reporting I'm on speed, or freaked-out. & avoiding the tenants, not answering when there's a knock on the door. & Mom called from Mackinac saying why didn't I come up after all, spend a few days it's so lovely here the water so beautiful & air so clear. & Dad came on the line hearty & friendly & ERASE with my thumb. & again Junie & I lift the phone & right away she's bitching. It's August 21 & why haven't I returned her calls, she'd left at least three messages for mc shc was worried about me for God's sake! & so on. I'm eating frozen Taco Bell beef burritos & drinking Bud out of the can. Flicking through the TV channels. Fifty-two channels & back again to the beginning. I'm edgy like there is something I am seeking & don't know what it is. Junie is TALKING. Like she's always TALKED. Big Sis who's hot shit, junior high principal. Gummy green guacamole sauce running down my arm. On channel six there's naked black corpses in a dump somewhere in Africa. On channel nine there's bawling children in some bombed-out hospital in this place called Bosnia. & fading to an ad *This is your governor speaking.* On channel eleven an ad for a van bouncing over a rocky desert landscape. On channel twelve the weather news *Michigan & Great Lakes region continued high temperatures.* On MTV a hot-looking spic cunt with electric hair is licking the nipples of a strung-out cokehead whitey & I'm flicking back to channel eleven. Junie is saying sharp like she's in the room with me *Quentin damn it are you there?* & Q__ says *Where the fuck else would I be, Junie?* & there's a pause like the bitch has been slapped in the face. & I'm trying to finish the burrito & staring at the TV screen knowing there is some message here, something urgent. Junie says she would like to speak with me, she *is* worried about me, the influence *the wrong kind of associates* can have on me. It's a new-model Dodge Ram speeding over the rocky terrain. Big glaring moon in the sky. Or is the Dodge Ram on the moon, & that's the Earth floating there? Junie is saying I owe it to Mom & Dad to try to live a good life. & I *am* a good decent person deep in my heart—she knows. Says she isn't always *on an emotional equilibrium* herself. She has her *stressed-out periods*, too. In fact she's seeing *a holistic therapist in Ann Arbor.* But please don't tell Mom & Dad, Quentin?—they think I'm the strong one. They depend on me to be there for *them*. A pause & she says Quentin? *are* you there? & I grunt yeah yeah & I'm thinking how your sister (or it could be your brother) comes out of the identical hole you came out of. & shot from the identical prick. & all of it blind & chance & yet there's the DNA CODE. & that is why a sister (or a brother) knows you that way you don't want to be known. Not that Junie knows *me*. Not that anybody in the Universe knows *me*. But if one of them did it would be Junie staring into Q__ P__'s soul.

Junie repeats she's inviting me for dinner tomorrow night, not just to talk but there's this friend she'd like me to meet & I say I'm busy. Well, the night after that?—& I'm busy. & she's pissed saying what's the big deal in *your* life, Quentin? don't bullshit *me*. Saying, you're involved with—who? & I'm watching TV & don't hear. & she says, serious now, You know what I'm afraid of, Quentin?—one of your *secret associates,* some druggie will injure you one of these days, that's what I'm afraid of. For Mom & Dad's sake. Because you're too naive & you're too trusting like it's the Sixties or something & you're too plain God-damned *stupid* to know your own best interests.

The Dodge Ram bounces over the landscape. Fade to assholes in baseball uniforms, Tiger Stadium, Detroit.

Now I know the final step. Eating the second burrito I'm not even hungry for but I'm ravenous, my mouth is alive by itself & devouring what's in my hand. On the way to GROUND ZERO in four days. Like a jigsaw puzzle part that's been missing & now I have it & the puzzle is complete.

Went down into the cellar & shut & locked the door behind me. & into the old cellar, & shut & secured the door. & there were the BABY CHICKS like I'd dreamt them except they were real! CHEEP CHEEP CHEEPING. & no fear of me. & I changed their water (in aluminum foil saucers) in each of the boxes & picked out some of the droppings & sprinkled bread pellets & grain for them. & though only a week or so old these BABY CHICKS pecked hungrily & unerringly & could take care of themselves like adult birds. For all their lives were just eating. & that was provided for them.

Counted them for the hell of it. Each cardboard box, twelve BABY CHICKS. Thirty-six BABY CHICKS. They were all still alive.

45

Next day, asked Grandma could I borrow $$$ for a down payment on a Dodge Ram?—my old Ford is so beat-up & the garage says it will cost more to repair (brakes & carburetor) than it is worth. & Grandma says *Quentin, of course!* & smiling & her bony hands trembling a little as she writes out the check. *It's a loan,* I say. *I will pay you back.* & Grandma laughs *Oh Quentin.* They want somebody to love & live for—women. It doesn't matter who like it would with a man. & for lunch preparing big grilled cheese sandwiches for me crossed with strips of crisp bacon I was crazy for as a boy visiting Grandma. & Grandma sips her piss-colored tea & takes her "heart pills" as she calls them. *I feel I've just gotten to know you, Quentin. This summer. God works in unexpected ways doesn't He!*

Saying, *This is just between you & me, Quentin. Our little secret!*

I'm hungry, & I'm eating. & the check in my shirt pocket. Since making my decision I've had the best appetite in years & needed a new notch in my belt this morning. On double 'ludes my heart is calm &

strong & pounding steady & the pulse of it sharp in my cock. GROUND ZERO so close it is almost like it *has* happened. & when I return to 118 North Church Street MY ZOMBIE SQUIRREL will be awaiting me in the cellar. Food & drink & a full-length mirror for his (& his master's) use. SQUIRREL's worshipful green eyes, & pigtail so sexy. & that MOUTH made for kisses & sucking. & that worshipful ASS. & Grandma is saying a tremor in her voice the only thing left to make her life complete, she would die happy then, if Junie or me, or both of us she loves so would get married & have children & the lineage would not die out. Such proud good upstanding decent Christian men & women were our ancestors Grandma says. & we go:

"Quentin?—nothing would make me happier."

"What's that, Grandma?"

"I said—nothing would make me happier, if you would marry one day soon, & have children." Brushing at her eyes & laughing sadly, saying, "I know I'm an old woman & it's none of my business to interfere with you young people's lives."

"No Grandma, that's O.K."

"I know it *is* too much to ask. Just to make an old woman happy."

"No Grandma, that's O.K."

"I know—the world is so different now."

& I'm licking cherry-swirl ice cream from the spoon looping my tongue around the spoon saying, "Grandma, hey no. Don't cry. The world is not ever that different."

46

HOW THINGS PLAY OUT. Purchased the Dodge Ram, Aug. 23. Cheated in the trade-in (got only $1300 for the Ford) but in no position to bargain. Dark green-brown finish & solid good-looking chassis standing higher from the ground, more macho than the Ford, & four-wheel drive of course. & more horsepower than the Ford, & roomier in the rear. Practiced driving it using gears, lights etc. & the air-conditioning system which is complicated. Purchased a dozen dark-green plastic garbage bags to tape over the rear windows & no American flag decal this time—maybe I will add one later. & a new bumper sticker I'D RATHER BE SAILING. Most of Aug. 24 laying in supplies in the cellar & cistern. Ice pick, dental pick, knives of varying sizes all newly sharpened. Iodine & gauze & bandages etc. Easy foods for SQUIRREL to eat & digest & Evian water & blankets & a piss-pot (a ceramic pot from up in the attic, might be an antique?) & toilet paper etc. & the full-length mirror (also from the attic). Also preparing the van. Securing a plywood partition between the second seat & the rear. In the back seat, another

T-shirt, a pair of jeans, box of Froot Loops for quick energy & more Evian water & three bottles of dago red in paper bags. Back of the van, gloves & sponge-gag & rolls of masking tape & rope & the burlap sack & waterproof canvas for the floor, & more garbage bags. I did not want the rear of my new van soiled. (There was no plan for blood to spill in the van, & I hoped that would not happen, but a specimen will panic even the bravest ones sometimes & lose bowel control.) & my fish-gutting knife. (My .38 pistol I would carry in my pocket.) & selected my TODD CUTTLER curly red-brown hair & smooth moustache not touched for years. Ate at Burger King up the street & stopped by a college tavern & had only a few beers & talked to no one & early to bed, only a single 'lude & slept like a baby. Aug. 25 woke 6:20 A.M. excited & cock like an electric baton & had to jerk off twice & the cum was hot as lava. Burger King Special Breakfast $3.99 & I cleaned my plate & had so much coffee I got a caffeine buzz & it felt good. Household chores as usual. Said hello etc. to Big Black Guy (who is always in the kitchen frying something dark & greasy in a pan) & I believe I handled him O.K. To make them think, if they hate whitey, you are *not* really whitey but something else. Showered & put on MT. VERNON U. T-shirt, white cotton with green letters & Indian tomahawk logo. Beltless khaki work-shorts, socks & jogging shoes. Called Grandma as planned. It is Thursday, I am expected to mow part of the lawn. But Grandma asked please would I pick up her dear friend Mrs. Thatch & bring her over?—for I had done so in the past, &

never minded. & so stammered O.K. & then it was too late. Then thinking *It might be better: two old women & not just one.* Continued preparations. Put on TV in my room & left, locking door. 4:40 P.M. & the house empty at this hour. Carried cartons of baby chicks up from the cellar & into the rear of the van pulled up close to the back door. Drove to Dale Springs along usual route & picked up Mrs. Thatch, 13 Lilac Lane at 5:00 P.M. Four-minute drive to Grandma's at 149 Arden. Old woman chattering non-stop saying *How lucky your grandmother is to have such a thoughtful grandson.* Baby chicks CHEEP CHEEP CHEEPING but behind the partition & the old woman is chattering too much to hear or is deaf. At Grandma's I drank lemonade, & after a few minutes left the two of them jabbering in the house & returned to move the van into a position beside the garage not visible from the house. & put on my Tigers cap & work gloves & pushed the mower out of the garage & began mowing rear of lawn at 5:25 P.M. moving as usual in swaths width-wise working from the house toward the rear. At 5:35 P.M. positioned mower behind an evergreen shrub about midway in the lawn & secured it & leaving the motor roaring crossed to the garage unseen from the house. In van, put on TODD CUTTLER hair & moustache & again Tigers cap. Dark sunglasses. At 5:52 P.M. drove slowly out of Grandma's driveway & west on Arden to Locust & north to the one-way al-ley below Lakeview Boulevard & along the alley to GROUND ZERO where parked, motor running. Alley deserted. In rear of van, final preparations. Opened

143

one of the rear doors & at 6:02 P.M. lowered cartons of baby chicks to the ground & at 6:03 P.M. opened cartons to release baby chicks. At once CHEEP CHEEP CHEEPING & fluttering their little wings spreading out from the cartons & pecking in the dirt oblivious to all save the dirt. & I remained calm & controlled. *For all that has happened, has happened. From the beginning of Time.* Approximately 6:08 P.M. sighted bicycle turning into the alley. Thereafter ceased to take note of precise time but remained calm, controlled. SQUIRREL pedaling in my direction as in my dreams. For how could he not. For what other destiny. & SQUIRREL staring in disbelief seeing the bright yellow Easter chicks so fluffy & cute in the alley in his path had no choice but to slow & brake his bike. & straddling his bike laughed saying *Hey what's up? Baby chicks?* & TODD CUTT-LER anxious & pissed says *I had an accident, they got loose, can you help me? Please!* & SQUIRREL who's a good-natured kid, unsuspecting & happy to be of use grinned and parked his bike saying *Sure!* Swooping down to catch two of the fluttering chicks in his hands & bringing them to TODD CUTTLER stooped over one of the cartons at the rear of the van. Saying *How'd you get so many? Wow! Wild!* like it's a joke, some fantasy of MTV maybe. & TODD CUTTLER smiled & said *Thanks!* & SQUIRREL turned to catch two more chicks near the rear right tire of the van & in that instant TODD CUTTLER quick as a snake slid a crushing forearm beneath the boy's chin & with his other arm pinioned the boy's thrashing arms & ONE TWO THREE hard jolts against the boy's

144

windpipe almost snapping his neck & he was out on his feet, legs limp & useless. & TODD CUTTLER within seconds lifted & hauled him inside the van, & the doors shut & locked. & TODD CUTTLER was aroused & fierce his eyes bulging in his head. & his cock enormous. & shoving the sponge into SQUIRREL's mouth & securing it with tape wound around his head & jaws. & pulled the burlap sack over SQUIRREL's head & secured that too with tape. & now the face & head were gone, & the boy's body lay shuddering with breath. & a stain darkening his crotch. & the smell of urine. & excited TODD CUTTLER fumbled & tore at the boy's jeans & exposed his soft damp cock & tore at his own clothes & ONE TWO THREE hard jolts into the boy's scrotum & moaning & his own eyes lurching in his head he came, & came. & there was a blackout of how many seconds, or minutes, he did not know. & laying upon the boy shuddering & trying to calm his heart. *I love you, don't make me hurt you. Love love love you!* & a wetness ran from his mouth like a baby's. & his eyes blinded with tears. & yet the burlap sack was scratchy against his heated skin. & the boy so thin beneath him, the rib cage & collarbone. & the boy revived & began weakly to groan inside the sponge & thrashing his arms & legs. & TODD CUTTLER lay his weight upon him to secure him. *Lay still & you won't be hurt! Lay still & you won't be hurt! I am your friend.* & the boy in terror was stronger than expected but TODD CUTTLER was stronger. Grunting & pinioning the boy's arms to his sides & winding around him a strip of burlap & securing it with rope like a straitjacket. & tying the boy's legs, ankles & calves & knees. & the boy could not now move except to writhe like an injured worm. Yet still he writhed, & deep in his throat a groaning wailing sound like a baby crying at a distance & this pissed TODD CUTTLER who straddled him & closed his fingers around the boy's neck where a pulse beat saying, panting *You won't be hurt! You won't be hurt I promise you! But don't FIGHT ME.* & TODD CUTTLER tightened his fingers & shook & shook the boy's head banging it against the floor of the van until seeing the boy was still & not resisting he crawled from him. & came to an awareness of where he was & the task that was his & the danger. For he seemed to have forgotten the danger. As at all such times. & staring at his wristwatch seeing the time now 6:23 P.M. & at first could not comprehend what this meant. Then recovering & removing the wig & moustache (which had come partway loose & hung down his lip) & adjusting his khaki shorts he'd opened. & examining the boy seeing he was breathing, his rib cage rising & falling in spasms. So it was O.K. & hurriedly climbing out of the van on the driver's side & into the driver's seat & checked the rearview mirror seeing the alley was still empty. & drove the van (the dashboard so strangely new & the steering tight & the bulk of the vehicle unexpected) in slow jerks at first & then more smoothly forward & through the church parking lot (which was almost empty, & nobody to as much as glance in his direction) & to Pearl Street & south to Arden & east on Arden to Grandma's. & there was no sound from the

146

rear. & parked the van as before. & locked all doors with the automatic lock. & tried to see into the rear but the dark green plastic strips blocked all vision. & hurried then to the mower *which was still roaring*. All this time, & *still roaring*. & the old women would've heard, & would believe I had been there. Returned to the mowing & took comfort in it as sometimes you do—back & forth, back & forth across the width of the lawn. & happening to see, glancing around—what was it?—A DOG SNIFFING AT THE VAN! A DOG!—& for a moment stood staring then clapped my hands & shouted for it to get away, & it stood staring at me for a moment & I yelled *Get home! Get away!* & the dog turned & trotted down the driveway. & went away. & at 6:54 P.M. I quit mowing & pushed the mower into the garage. Checked the van in the driveway seeing it seemed O.K. & no sound from the rear. Went into the house & told Grandma I was done for today, the back lawn was mowed. It was 7:00 P.M. & I had to leave. & Grandma & the other old woman looked at me. & Grandma said, *Quentin, your face,* & I said *What about my face?* & Grandma said, *You look over-heated, dear, why don't you wash up.* So I washed up. & saw in the bathroom mirror Q__ P__ looking at me dazed & sunburnt-seeming. & a vein of blood in the left eye. & the hairline receding. *What of your future, son?—you are over thirty years old.* & the beer gut, & tight belt if I'd worn a belt which I did not, with these khaki shorts. & returned to the kitchen where Grandma & the other old woman were talking about Q__ P__, I know. & it crossed my

147

mind I might kill them both now, & the other one out in the van, & dispose of the three corpses at once & that would save time, & I wouldn't have to think about it anymore. Grandma saying, *Oh Quentin but can't you stay for dinner* & I said. & Grandma said *Oh but I wish you would! I don't think you eat right, living alone. A bachelor's life is a hard one.* & I said should I drive Mrs. Thatch home now. & Mrs. Thatch was staying for dinner it seemed & said oh no she would take a taxi home. & I was moving toward the door & Grandma cried *Oh Quentin wait!* & gave me an envelope which would contain $$$ & I took it & thanked her & left. & at the van, which was the new shining green-brown Dodge Ram & not the other, THERE WAS THE DOG AGAIN—a skinny breed with stringy hair & curving tail like a monkey's, & alert eyes & I shouted *Get away! Fuck off!* & clapped my hands & kicked at it, & it ran away. Was it SQUIRREL's dog? My .38 pistol in my pocket, should I kill the dog? No sound inside the van. Got inside, & backed out of the driveway crooked & onto the lawn but on the street drove O.K., the steering wheel was sort of tight in the new van & the bulk of the van clumsy. But I was O.K. It was 7:12 P.M. West in slow traffic along Lakeview to the lake. These hours of Q__ P__'s plan before returning to 118 North Church in the darkness had never been worked out clearly I realized & were but a blur. As in a movie there is a FADE OUT, & a FADE IN to a later time. But I could not do that. I did not have that power. I was *in* Time. & the clock lacking hands, & stuck. & the Dodge Ram burning gas faster than the Ford. *You might be a little surprised, be prepared for the price of a full tank when you gas up* the salesman said. But I could not think of that now. Parked in Summit Park overlooking the lake & ate Froot Loops, for I was hungry, & drank from one of the wine bottles cautious to keep it hidden in the bag. For what if a cop saw, & came to question me. & the .38 pistol in my pocket I could not use in safety because the sound of the shot would be heard. Because that is the weakness of a gun, & why a knife is superior. But to kill any living thing with a knife is not easy. You would want to avoid it if you could. The sun was still high in the sky above the lake & I thought *It will never get dark*. A ridge of dark ragged cloud like broken teeth at the edge of the lake, & brighter sky above. & my ZOMBIE a burden to me & not the joy I had expected. & I finished the first bottle, & must've dozed behind the wheel, & woke hearing a snort which was out of my own throat. & still the day was light! & the sun glaring above the same ridge of cloud. Like a blind eye, yet it is still glaring. & the waves of Lake Michigan lapping & tepid in the heat. Toxin-waves Junie said. What have we done to nature! Junie said. *She will look into your eyes & know: & what must you do?* I turned to stare at the plywood partition behind the seats & it was—just there. & no sound beyond. & for a moment could not remember who was back there—which one of my specimens. For everything that happens, has happened. & will happen again. & remembering then the boy climbing out of the swimming pool—so shining with life. & began to feel revived again, & excited. For he was *mine* now, & always will be so. In sickness & in health & till Death depart. So started the motor & drove through the picnic area, so many people! families! so many kids! the smell of charcoal-grilled meat, & slowly through the park & this weird thought came *Yes but you could release him even now, dump him into the woods & somebody would find him. For it is TODD CUTTLER he saw, & not Q__ P__.* But I was pissed with him. Always you get pissed with them, & want to punish. Taunting me & following me in my head all these weeks. Looking through me in the Humpty Dumpty like there was nobody where I sat. & provoking me, that sidelong dimple-smile & green eyes. & I was driving south into Mt. Vernon along the lake & began to feel a warning. & turned on the radio to listen for news, for it was 8:08 P.M. now & by now SQUIRREL would be missed. & maybe the police had been notified? & beginning to search, & set up roadblocks? There was nothing on the news. But that might've been a trick. Yet I could not return home till nighttime, & dark. *& there is where you fuck up, Quen-tin, for all your plans.* I heard the mockery in Dad's voice yet did not blame him. & so decided suddenly I would turn, & drive north of the city after all, on Route 31 familiar to me as my own face. & so past Holland, & past Muskegon & by 9:20 P.M. & darkness I was beyond Ludington & in the Manistee Forest & feeling O.K. knowing I had made a right decision. For it had not been so, what I had told Dad's lawyer. That the Mt. Vernon cops cruised North Church & harassed me. Yet it seemed now so obvious it *was* so. & I did not know it. & SQUIRREL's disappearance in Dale Springs would alert the police to *known sex offenders* in that area. & how many would there be—dozens, a hundred. & Q__ P__ on the computer with these. & so it was shrewd to escape Mt. Vernon, & I parked on the side of a forest trail & went into the rear of the van & the light came on & the smell of urine stung my nostrils & excited me & I saw the body, the boy, flat on his back on the floor, head hidden in the burlap sack, part naked & his skinny rib cage moving *still breathing! still alive.* I had crushed something in his throat I believe—windpipe? larynx? & so tied him with tape & rope it was like a child would tie somebody, wound round & round. *Hello* I said. *Hi.* Squatted over him & touched & caressed & stroked but the little penis was limp & cool like a dead thing, I squeezed it to rouse some life in him & his muscles jerked & he seemed to cry out inside the sponge. I yanked off the burlap sack—& there was his face. *His* face, but changed. & not so good-looking now. The lower part of his face was taped over but the eyes fluttered open. *Now you see my true face, now you know your Master.* Splashed Evian water on him & a focus came into his eyes & I saw the terror in them. *I won't hurt you, I am your friend. If you don't fight me.* My voice tender & cajoling. Yet he did not seem to hear. There was the terror in his eyes, & the tension in his body tight as a board. A homely kid with blood-caked nostrils, I was getting pissed at him. His cock shriveled so tiny, like a ten-year-old's, & that look in his eyes. & thrashing his head, & trying again to fight—to fight *me*!—weak as a broken worm. MY ZOMBIE. FIGHTING *ME*. & losing control then I turned him over onto his belly & straddling him & gripping the little pigtail banging his face against the floor & fucking him in the ass my cock enormous so the skin tore & bled, ONE TWO THREE thrusts piercing to his guts like a sword *Who's your Master? Who's your Master? WHO'S YOUR MASTER?*

47

Do bones float?

    & if so, but no flesh is attached, & the bones themselves scattered & lost to one another, what *identity* is there. I never think of it.

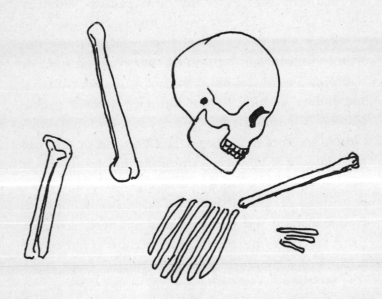

48

Aug. 26 & I was no sooner home & out of the shower & beginning my CARETAKER tasks for the day than the loud knocking came at the front door. & I knew.

I had not listened to any news reports. For why should Q__ P__ have listened. It was 7:50 A.M. I did not know anything, I was not aware of anything. But freshly shaven & my thinning hair combed sleek & damp against my skull & my eyes veined with red but hiding nothing behind my clear-framed plastic glasses. Wearing a clean plain white-cotton T-shirt, old chino work-pants, sandals. (It would be another hot-humid day.) & heard the knocking on the front door & that crackling sound of a police radio, a police squad car pulled into the driveway behind the Dodge Ram. I did not look but I knew. & heard the door being unlocked & opened, it was one of the tenants on his way out & there on the front steps two Mt. Vernon police officers. & their voices asking after Q__ P__ was he a resident of this house? & I stood cold & paralyzed in the hall thinking of the cistern! the dinette "operating" table! the surgical supplies! the store of food, & blankets, & the full-length mirror! & in the CARETAKER's quarters the Polaroid-mementos of my failed ZOMBIES, & the memento in formaldehyde of BIG GUY, & other items no eyes but Q__ P__'s must ever see. The Dodge Ram I had taken care to cleanse as thoroughly as possible, before dawn working frantically barefoot & bare-chested washing away all evidence. For there was little blood *in* the van, mainly piss & the lingering stink of piss. My soiled clothes, wig etc. I had shredded & buried in such scattered sites along Route 31, Q__ P__ himself could never recall. & my .38 pistol, the knives & my solitary memento of SQUIRREL I had placed in safekeeping far from 118 North Church.

Yet there was no choice but to come forward, & declare *Yes I am Q__ P__*. & calm & quizzical approaching the police officers at the door, one uniformed & the other in suit & tie. Greeted me & asked would I step outside. But I did not. Nor did I invite them inside. For this was not like the arrest after the black boy ran bellowing into the street when they dragged me from the van & threw me on my belly & face in the dirt & cuffed my wrists behind my back so I screamed in pain. This was not an actual arrest—was it? But only a questioning. For there were many names on the computer, *known sex offenders.* For they had no evidence, & they had no warrant or they would already be at their search. *Don't let them inside the house,* Dad's lawyer had said. *Don't go anywhere with them voluntarily. If they continue to harass you, call me. Any hour of the night or day—*

call me. They were asking could they come inside & I shook my head no, I did not think so. They were polite asking again would I step outside & I was polite & reasonable saying, trying not to stammer, I did not think so. & this surprised them, who are accustomed to bullying citizens. I asked them what did they want? & they looked at me, the older of them in the suit & tie sucking his lip, *You know what we want, son, don't you,* & I shook my head no, no I did not, & steeled myself looking at his eyes, & I saw no certainty in them, nor in the face of the other. & this went on for several minutes. & what I knew was that I knew, & they did not. & that I knew of my rights as a citizen. & would not acquiesce to police harassment of a man on probation, who has not violated probation. & a man who is "gay" & docs not advertise the fact but is not ashamed of it either, & guilty of nothing because of it either. & at last they spoke of a "young boy" who had been "abducted" the evening before in Dale Springs & he was missing & his bicycle found in an alley & they only wanted to ask a few questions of me, what I might know of this or might have heard, etc., here or at the precinct station, & if I had no objection they would like to look around the premises a little. & I shook my head & repeated no I did not think so, my lawyer has advised me to call him if there is trouble of any kind from the police, if I am harassed in any way & I would like to call him now.

& there was a silence. & the cops stood & stared at me, & I remained inside the doorway not surrendering an inch.

The detective said, *All right, son. Call your lawyer. Call him right now. & we'll be right out here.*

So I called Dad's lawyer at his home. & my voice young & aggrieved as a kid's telling him of this latest harassment. For an "abduction" I did not know of, having not watched the news, & could they arrest me? with no evidence, arrest me? & Dad's lawyer spoke to soothe me saying what my rights were, though I should not try to leave the premises. No doubt they were waiting for a search warrant. From where I stood in my room now I could see the two of them plus another, uniformed cop in the driveway contemplating the Dodge Ram that shone so in the sun, circling it & peering into the back (I had removed the plywood partition of course & the strips of plastic from the windows) & seeing—what? Nothing. There was nothing to see. Yet they did not dare break into the van for fear, if they did discover evidence, they would have seized it illegally, & it would be of no worth.

Dad's lawyer said he would be over immediately, & not to speak any further to the police above all not to volunteer any information however innocent nor allow them any entry, & I told him O.K., & hung up. How much time did I have! When would they break in! First thing I did was flush NO-NAME's gold tooth down the toilet, out of my pocket & gone forever. & the next, grabbing the formaldehyde bottle out of the locker & going next-door into the kitchen saying to two of the tenants waiting for a tea kettle to boil I was going to fumigate the kitchen, sorry they would

157

have to step out for a few minutes for safety's sake but the kettle could remain on the stove etc. So they went out, it was Akhil & a young Egyptian chemistry student, & I dumped BIG GUY into the kitchen sink & with a knife stabbed & cut & forced it into the garbage disposal & set the disposal going with a high grinding roar. & the formaldehyde poured down the drain, making my eyes sting & I was close to puking, & shook Dutch Cleanser into the sink & scrubbed with a steel wool pad, & after that Drāno down the disposal, & into the quart bottle too, to counteract the powerful stink of the chemical, & I believe it did. & another time running the disposal, grinding up just chunks of hand soap & it was all smooth & clean & smelled of something clean. & the tea kettle was boiling & singing, so I took it off the heat, & called Akhil & his friend back, & said the fumigation was over, & I did not think they were in any danger now. Back in my room then (I could see the cops still in the driveway—FUCKERS! Wanted to yell out the window at them FUCKERS! HARASSING me & SCREWING UP my life!) tearing up the map of SQUIRREL's bike route & the Polaroids & burnt them in my bathroom sink & washed the ashes down the drain & again scrubbed with steel wool. & downstairs in the old cellar dragged the dinette out of the cistern, & into the new cellar. Set a plastic laundry basket on it. & giant box of Tide. The ice pick & knives I brought up into the kitchen & tossed in a drawer with such utensils. & the sharp little silver pick Q__ P__ had pocketed from Dr. Fish's office went into my medicine cabinet with toothbrush, flossing string etc., for this was the logical place & I did not wish to lose such a valuable instrument. For there were other specimens awaiting I did not doubt, & I would not be harassed & intimidated by those fuckers into surrendering my rights. The bandages, gauze, etc. went into a supply closet in the pantry, & the food & Evian water. The mirror I dragged into the new cellar & propped in a corner with some old furniture. In the mirror Q__ P__ oily-faced & sullen & his hairline God-damn receding for sure, light winking off his glasses. *A responsible man makes his own luck.* But I was pissed.

A relief, Mom & Dad are up north. When they learn of this humiliation, it will be all over.

Dad's lawyer arrived, & not long after another squad car & the fuckers had a search warrant & could not be stopped. Two began with the Dodge Ram—I had no choice but to hand over the keys—& the rest with the house. & the lawyer stipulated that the search must be confined to certain areas only for this was a rental property & the rooms of the individual tenants are private & must not be ravaged by a search. & so they searched the CARETAKER's quarters of course, making a mess, & all of the cellar & the attic, & the downstairs rooms, closets, etc. & FOUND NOTHING. FOR THERE WAS NOTHING TO FIND.

That day too I was questioned about the missing boy whose name was new & unknown to me— *James,* or *"Jamie," Waldron.* Dad's lawyer was present of course, so my rights were protected. Because Q__ P__ knew nothing about the boy, & could only

159

repeat & repeat a few facts. That I had done yard work at Grandma's, from 5 P.M. until 7 P.M. & had afterward driven to Summit Park hoping to cool off & had had something to eat at McDonald's close by & then—for it had come to me in a brainstorm, of course they would check the odometer in the new Dodge Ram & note the mileage—I had driven along the lake, & in the University Heights area, for a long time, *hoping to get cool.* By this time Dad's lawyer had contacted Grandma, & Mrs. Thatch, to corroborate that I had been at Grandma's for the hours stated, & both were adamant that this was so. Grandma said her grandson was the kindest & most thoughtful young man on earth, he visited her often & did favors not only for her but for her friends. & since the time of the boy's abduction had been fixed between 6 P.M. when he left his place of employment & 6:40 P.M. when his bicycle was discovered abandoned in an alley a mile from his home, *it could not be* that Q__ P__ was in any way involved.

There was the mystery, too, of the baby chicks in the alley. No one living nearby could identify or claim them. No one had ever seen baby chicks in such a place before. Nor were there any grown hens anywhere in the neighborhood. The detective spoke quizzically of this fact, THIRTY-SIX BABY CHICKS loose & picking in the dirt of the alley, & the missing boy's expensive bicycle parked nearby with its kickstand down. Which suggested that he was not snatched from the bicycle, but accompanied his abductor, or whoever it was, willingly. What connection could there be between the missing boy & the baby chicks! *Or maybe there was no connection, at all?* Q__ P__ sat silent & frowning & had nothing to say, for he had no idea. The lawyer said skeptically, *Maybe the boy was playing a joke, & isn't missing. Some kind of fraternity prank.*

The detective in suit & tie sucked at his lip & said, *If it is, it isn't very funny. Is it?*

The cops were finished with their search upstairs & down, & went out. It was 12:40 P.M. I had not eaten anything since before 6 A.M., Froot Loops washed down with shitty-warm Evian water driving home on Route 31 from the Manistee Forest. From the unnamed narrow & deep & fast-flowing river where my fucked-up ZOMBIE SQUIRREL lay at the bottom naked & his throat slashed entering the water so the water bore the blood away into such an infinity it could never be traced, & his skinny body weighed down with burlap & rocks & would never rise except when the bones fall away from one another, released of flesh & identity. There would be the skull & the teeth of the skull they say you can identify—BUT COULD A SKULL FLOAT? I don't think a skull could float, being too heavy.

The sponge-gag, the strips of tape around his jaws I had left in place. In the end, I worked fast.

The detective said thanks & goodbye for now & did not seem sarcastic but only tired. & out in the driveway I saw him talking with one of the younger men, in uniform. & I interrupted the lawyer who was speaking of *suing for harassment* if more of this ensued, & said, "Maybe—maybe I could t-talk to them, after all."

161

"Excuse me?"

"The police. Maybe I could talk to them, after all." I was swallowing hard, my throat so dry. I did not make EYE CONTACT with Dad's lawyer. "Just for a m-minute, by myself?"

The lawyer was looking at Q__ P__ like he had not seen me before. & did not like what he saw. His head was the shape of a light bulb & pale & almost hairless, the hairs in thin crimped strips. He was Dad's age & I believe a friend of Dad's from some other time when they were all young. He said, "Are you out of your mind? Absolutely not."

"O.K.," I said.

49

Labor Day, & a few days later. Junie called & left a message on the tape. Did I see the morning paper. What a shock—the news about Dr. M__ K__.

Daddy will be devastated Junie said.

Didn't get around to listening to the message for a few days, & by that time that day's newspaper was gone. I wasn't even sure which day it was.

50

Labor Day, & the fall term starting at the University. & of our nine tenants five are new, just moving in. All of them foreign students. Graduate students in the sciences mostly. From India, China, Pakistan, Zaire, Egypt, West Indies. Dad says they make the best tenants & he is right. All dark-skinned, & polite & shy & speaking our language with care. I am Q__ P__ CARETAKER & introduced to them as such.

I am taking my medication again as Dr. E__ prescribes. Three times daily with meals. & to help me sleep when required. You are not supposed to *ingest alcohol* while on lithium but that has not been a problem for me. The purpose is to *maintain emotional equilibrium* as Dr. E__ says.

Feeling low lately. Since GROUND ZERO etc. Bummed. But don't think of it, & the medication helps. That is its purpose. & no point in blaming others, like Dad or Grandma. (I have stopped yard work at Grandma's house for the indefinite future. & driving Grandma around like a taxi service. Fuck that *grandson crap.* It only gets you into trouble.)

Jean-Paul from the West Indies, white shirt &

a wild Afro, shorts, sandals, muscled oxblood-shining calves. Came up to Q__ P__ at Burger King & said hello, so friendly. Grad student with a fellowship in economics. So quick & friendly I could not prevent EYE CONTACT. But it will not be repeated.

Nor any of them beneath this roof. I never think of it.

51

Mon. 4:00 P.M.–4:50 P.M. Mt. Vernon Medical Center on the other side of the campus, in good weather I walk & in bad weather drive the Dodge Ram. Dr. E__ says *Well, Quen-tin. This brisk autumn air is a tonic isn't it. After our long hot summer.*

There is a double meaning in this I know. *Summer* the time of Q__ P__'s harassment & humiliation by Mt. Vernon Police Department. But I smile & say YES DOCTOR. NO DOCTOR. Sit & smile & my hair cut & parted in a new way. Dad's lawyer requested reports to the Michigan Probation Department & so it is known by us that Dr. E__'s prognosis of his patient Q__ P__ is "very good." Q__ P__ is "definitely making progress."

Still it is awkward in Dr. E__'s office. I sit across from his desk & stare at the floor. Or at my hands I have scrubbed. RAISINEYES' wristwatch on my left arm & its bronze face secret where I watch the tiny numerals flashing bronze. & around my right wrist my solitary memento of SQUIRREL.

Dr. E__ asks do I have any dreams to speak of today. There is a flurry of leaves against the window behind him & the sky is darkening so early. I sit & frown & an oily sweat on my forehead & upper lip & there is a long silence. Then I say, *A dream of being in some water.* & Dr. E__ says *Yes? What of it?* & I can't think of more & he says encouraging me like you would encourage a little child to speak, *Are you swimming in this water, Quentin?* & I shake my head saying, *I don't think so, maybe I am just in the water. & the water hides me & carries me along.* & Dr. E__ says, *& what happens in your dream, Quentin?* & I say, *I don't know. I'm just there.*

There is peace too in Dr. E__'s office. You can take comfort in. Dad & Mom are pleased with their son's *prognosis* & hope that I will continue with Dr. E__ after my probation is over. Junie too has said in that stern solid way of hers there is *definitely an improvement in Quen.*

At last it is 4:19 P.M. Dr. E__ writes out a refill for my prescription. Asks if I have anything to ask him & I can't think of anything & THANK YOU DOCTOR & the session is over.

52

For all that has happened, has happened. From the beginning of Time. I accept this.

Alternate Thursdays 10 A.M. Mr. T__ my probation officer. Tues. 7 P.M.–8:30 P.M. group therapy with Dr. B__. Mon. & Thurs. trash pick-up. Dragging the yellow plastic trash pails out to the curb.

There is a change in my life: I am no longer enrolled at Dale Tech but have transferred to University Extension (downtown Mt. Vernon campus). INTRO TO ACCOUNTING Mon. & Wed. 7 P.M.–8:20 P.M. Because R__ P__ is on the University faculty my tuition is only $200. I am paying for it myself.

A new drive-through McDonald's is opening on Third St. just two blocks from 118 North Church. Bright yellow banners flapping in the wind & SPE-CIAL BIG MAC COUPONS to early customers. A glimpse of Jean-Paul in one of the booths with a woman, I think. Light-skinned & Jean-Paul is that deep russet-black. But I did not see clearly. I was not looking, & was not seen.

53

A true ZOMBIE would be mine forever. He would obey every command & whim. Saying "Yes, Master" & "No, Master." He would kneel before me lifting his eyes to me saying, "I love you, Master. There is no one but you, Master."

& so it would come to pass, & so it would be. For a true ZOMBIE could not say a thing that was *not,* only a thing that *was.* His eyes would be open & clear but there would be nothing inside them *seeing.* & nothing behind them *thinking.* Nothing *passing judgment.*

Nor would there be *terror* in my ZOMBIE's eyes. Nor *memory.* For without *memory* there is no *terror.*

A ZOMBIE would pass no judgment of course. A ZOMBIE would say, "God bless you, Master." He would say, "You are good, Master. You are kind & merciful." He would say, "Fuck me in the ass, Master, until I bleed blue guts." He would beg for his food & he would beg for oxygen to breathe. He would be respectful at all times. He would lick with his tongue as bidden. He would suck with his mouth as bidden. He would spread the cheeks of his ass as bidden. He would cuddle like a teddy bear as bidden. He would rest his head on my shoulder like a baby. Or I would rest my head on his shoulder like a baby. We would lie beneath the covers in my bed in the CARETAKER's room listening to the November wind & the bells of the Music College tower chiming & WE WOULD COUNT THE CHIMES UNTIL WE FELL ASLEEP AT EXACTLY THE SAME MOMENT.

54

Junie said, *Don't speak of it to Dad. His heart is broken.*

& Mom said, *Your father has aged twenty years! But when you see him, don't let on.*

The news did not seem important to me, no more than most news you see on TV or read in the paper. It was in fact news of long ago. & Dr. M__ K__ dead & spared any trouble. NOBEL LAUREATE FOUND TO HAVE LED RADIATION EXPERIMENTS 1953–1957. COMPARED TO "NAZI" DOCTORS.

I saw the photo of white-haired Dr. K__ Dad's old mentor at the Washington Institute & read of the scandal as they called it in the media. Dr. K__ had led a team of scientists who engaged in secret experiments for the Atomic Energy Commission. In one experiment, radioactive milk was fed to thirty-six mentally retarded children at a school in Bethesda, Maryland. In another, the testicles of prisoners at several Virginia universities were exposed to "ionizing radiation." Why this old news was revealed now so many years later & why people pretended to give a fuck, I don't know. But I had to laugh.

Lucky for Dad & Mom they were still on Mackinac Island when the scandal broke. Newspapers & TV & *People* & *Time* etc. Dad was spared the embarrassment of interviewers telephoning him & asking for a statement. Later he went on record saying *It is an unconscionable act to experiment on any person without informed consent but I knew Dr. K__ & I am unable to believe that he is guilty of such. There must be some mistake.* In private saying *So unfair to a dead man!* Dad removing his glasses & rubbing his hands over his eyes. & his tweed asshole mouth screwed up in pain. *A great man's reputation slandered posthumously, how can he defend himself!*

Of this I have not spoken to Dad, nor will. There is not that kind of easiness between us. Or Dad speaking to me about the police harassment at the time of the *Waldron boy's* disappearance.

But Dad removed the framed photos of Dr. M__ K__ & himself from his office at the University, & from home. If Grandma still has hers on the dining room wall I don't know. I never go to Grandma's any more. Nor to Dale Springs at all except sometimes to borrow $$$ from Mom.

55

A day is long & so the time has been long. Since
GROUND ZERO. I stay close to the house as CARE-
TAKER of the property. As Dad & Mom have entrusted me. Except some weekends driving in the
Dodge Ram (which holds the road so well, & has a
look of such pride) to Detroit on I-96 & once along
Lake Erie to Toledo where I had never been before.
& Ann Arbor where the University is even bigger
than Mt. Vernon, a Gay Pride Festival in October. Returning on I-94 in the early dawn perhaps & the sky
lightening in weird rosy-gray pleats & puckers &
there are bright orange markers flying at me CON-
STRUCTION AHEAD FORM SINGLE LANE 40 MPH but it is too
early & the highway is deserted. & the THUMP
THUMP THUMP of the pavement like a heartbeat.
Like the Dodge Ram & Q__ P__ have a single heartbeat. & I suppose I am happy, or anyway at peace. &
sometimes hitch-hikers. *Did not want it to happen
but our eyes met. & him high, & horny, & panting
like a stallion. & in the filthy lavatory at the rest
stop COMING so it was like scalding lava.* & once
in November feeling restless took the van north on

Rt. 31 to the Manistee Forest. & it was snowing & so the landscape was altered. Like a new place or even a planet where I could not get my bearings. Could not find the road I had taken with SQUIRREL & so could not find the river. Got turned around, & pissed as hell mistaking east for west (but there are no direct roads) & ended up at Big Rapids the opposite edge of the Forest. Most days now I am on my medication as Dr. E__ prescribes. Three tablets daily, with meals. This causes my words to slur sometimes & drowsiness driving & in INTRO TO ACCOUNTING where I sit at the back of the room. But my temper is O.K. & I am not so angry & EYE CONTACT does not worry me. If it is ACCIDENT & not deliberate (on my part). Akhil coming to my door for instance & saying, *Excuse me sir there is something wrong with the upstairs toilet I think.*

Jean-Paul who is new to the house & is always asking questions, for instance downstairs in the cellar where there is a washing machine & drier OFF LIMITS to tenants but I allowed him to use it one day, with the promise he would not tell the other tenants. & needing the CARETAKER to help him every step of the way. *I am used to a woman taking care of my laundry* Jean-Paul says laughing.

Most nights I don't go out, can't afford it. Begging for fucking crumbs from Mom & Dad. Eating takeout from Burger King, Taco Bell, etc. & drinking sixpacks watching XXX videos. Or TV flicking through the channels. It is hard to watch one channel for more than twenty seconds, or ten. Many times in the fall seeing *Mr. & Mrs. Waldron the parents of the missing "Jamie"* making their appeal on Michigan TV. & photos of "Jamie" & actual video-footage, home movies. & there was SQUIRREL smiling & waving at me, & SQUIRREL playing basketball at school, & SQUIRREL getting some kind of trophy. & a voice-over saying *Please if you have any information please contact hot-line JAMIE a $50,000 reward is offered for any information leading to the discovery of* & Mr. & Mrs. Waldron saying always the same words *We have faith that our son is still alive, we have faith that we will see him again, alive* & now Mrs. Waldron is crying & Mr. Waldron trying not to cry. & I'm losing it saying, loud & disgusted, *What do you mean—alive? Why should he be alive? Why the fuck should HE be alive?* & saying *Fuckers, now YOU know.* & flicking past the channel in disgust.

In November around Thanksgiving an unexpected news bulletin on local TV, someone claiming to have "sighted" the missing boy hitch-hiking in Chicago. But nothing came of this so far as I know.

56

Junie has been BIG SIS all my life. She is five years my elder. & as tall, & weighing maybe as much. Almost made the Olympics team as a swimmer in college, & was a star at *women's lacrosse.* Now PRINCIPAL at Dale Springs Middle School.

Junie has always taken an interest in Q__ the kid brother. Her only sibling in the family. In high school when I had some emotional problems & the year I started college at Eastern Michigan & screwed up. It was Junie's idea for me to study real estate & not return to college as Dad was always pushing saying college is not right for everyone. Saying Quen could be a terrific salesman if he'd only *lighten up.*

Left a message on the phone saying *Accounting is a great idea, Quen. A hell of a lot more realistic than those other ideas of Dad's.*

Mom & Dad are proud of Junie & have been so since high school when she was a class officer & star athlete. Graduated fifth in her class, 1976. & a scholarship to U.M. to study public education & administration, Ann Arbor the classy state school not second- & third-rate like Lansing & Mt. Vernon. & at college did pretty well. & now a principal & ambitious to move elsewhere, taking summer "seminars" etc. at Ann Arbor. Junie is "social" & has lots of friends, the kind you go hiking with, or skiing. When Junie bought her own house, on the lake in a suburb called Graafschap Mom worried *Now Junie will never get married.* Junie has gone through stages of being pissed as hell at her kid brother Q__ & not speaking to me & one time (I was drunk or in some state not 100% conscious, in my leather clothes & ponytail) not acknowledging me when we ran into each other on the street. But since the arrest & the two-years' probation when Mom & Dad were so upset, Junie has gone into gear as BIG SIS again. Like having a *sex offender* for a kid brother is a challenge to her, & she is not one to back off from challenges. Like I am one of her problem students only needing to be redeemed by some adult. Like I am somebody you can tease & nag with a smile saying *Quen, you'd be really good-looking if you didn't mope so much. & stand taller for God's sake. & can't you do something about your hair, & your clothes?*

Invited me to her place for a dinner, two weeks before Christmas. Some friends of hers I'd met before I think, though maybe not—Junie's teacher-friends look all alike. & talk alike. & a new faculty member at Junie's school named LUCILLE. Another big woman with tits like hub-caps & a round smiling face & lots of "personality" like Junie. Teaches eighth grade. Handshake like a man's.

It's a dinner sitting at a table. Big seafood "paella"

Junie made. & white wine. I arrived in the Dodge Ram a little late drinking en route, & mellowed out on 'ludes & this soft buzzing in my head like a dial tone. So I can tune out, & my face seems like I am listening. Junie & "Lucille" & the others all animated talking of politics in the state & in Washington, Clinton's health plan & etc. & one guy, runty but talking like he's sure of himself saying health care is the number one issue of our time, & we are not a civilized nation at present, & somebody else saying crime is the number one issue, Americans have become terrified of being victimized & are thus susceptible to dangerous right-wing paranoid politics. & from there to gun control, & abortion. & I'm O.K. drinking wine & I can see my cellar & cistern I have returned to their state before the cops came to harass me. Dinette table back in the cistern, & extension cord & 150-watt lights & the bandages, gauze etc. Ice pick, dental pick, knife, etc. & waiting for a plan to form. & excited knowing it will form, like a dream. *No specimen beneath this roof. Forbidden.* Except say it's the start of vacation, or one of them is returning home for good. To India, to Zaire, to the West Indies. O.K.? & he's all packed & his room cleared etc. & Q__ P__ CARETAKER volunteers to drive him to the airport. Not Kalamazoo but Lansing, the international airport. O.K.? & that's cool, & kind. & as far as anybody in the house or at the University knows, he's gone. Left the United States. & they don't think of him anymore, he's history. & on the way to the airport Q__ P__ gives him something to drink or eat & he falls asleep & the van is prepared again for a passenger in the rear & that's cool. & after dark we return to 118 North Church. & it's the middle of the night, & everybody asleep. & Q__ P__ carries his ZOMBIE down into the cellar & the door is locked behind him. & on the operating table the first procedure this time is not the *transorbital lobotomy* but "severing" the vocal cords. So if the ZOMBIE is O.K. or not he will at least be silent & trustworthy in that way. & I will get a diagram of the larynx or whatever it is from the biology library. & if I use a razor maybe. A light touch. *You can feel them. They vibrate when you speak.*

Junie & her friends are talking about religion now I guess. & one of the men says religion is tyranny, & delusion. & responsible for much of the cruelty of mankind. & Lucille all huffy & excited saying no that is *not* religion, that is power, political power, & religion is *spiritual, & inward.* & Junie agrees & she's excited too saying the struggle of our species is between *outward & political, & inward & spiritual.* & maybe the upcoming millennia will be the salvation of Homo sapiens. & I'm listening & watching them. Big Sis & Lucille. & the idea comes to me: if you sliced off a female's breasts she would then be not much different than a man, say if you sliced off a man's cock he would not be much different than a woman. The breasts are mainly fatty—no bones? & Lucille sees me looking at her & she's blushing a little like women do. & seeing me turning my wristband round & round sort of compulsive like I do she asks what is it?—my memento of SQUIRREL which is part of his blond-brown hair from his little pigtail & some

of my own hairs braided together with leather
thongs & red yarn.

So I say, "It's an Indian thing. Chippewa. I got it at
the reservation upstate."

& Lucille says, touching it, "It's *unusual*. Does it
have any symbolic meaning? Is it some Chippewa
custom?"

& I say, "I guess so. I don't know."

& Junie butts in dry & teasing, Big Sis reaching
over to lay a hand on me too, "Quen is some kind of
hippie, you know? Born thirty years too late."

& Lucille is smiling saying, "His hair is too short
for a hippie's."

& Junie says, "It didn't used to be, though."

Mom called & left a message & the answering tape screwed up & erased most of it. Asking would I come for Christmas dinner probably.